Parachute-
Ghosts

ROY POND

Paddle-Ghosts

AN ALBATROSS BOOK

© Roy Pond 1992

Published in Australia and New Zealand by
Albatross Books Pty Ltd
PO Box 320, Sutherland
NSW 2232, Australia
in the United States of America by
Albatross Books
PO Box 131, Claremont
CA 91711, USA
and in the United Kingdom by
Lion Publishing plc
Peter's Way, Sandy Lane West
Littlemore, Oxford OX4 5HG, England

First edition 1992

National Library of Australia
Cataloguing-in-Publication data

Pond, Roy
Paddle-Ghosts

ISBN 0 7324 1001 0 (Albatross)
ISBN 0 7459 2436 0 (Lion)

I. Title

A823.3

Cover illustration: Michael Mucci
Printed and bound in Australia by The Book Printer, Victoria

Contents

1 River ghosts   7

2 The PS Return   17

3 The past awakened   28

4 Playing games   36

5 The skipper   46

6 Lockmaster of time   58

7 River of snags   63

8 Willow tears   72

9 Mist of uncertainty   87

10 River of surprises   100

11 River of dew   111

12 Paddle-Ghost   116

13 Emma Jane's father   128

14 Friends of the PS Return   136

15 Back in the flow   142

1

River ghosts

THE SOFTLY TRAMPING PADDLEWHEEL at the stern of their houseboat marched them along at a steady ten knots through the haze of afternoon.

Matt stood alone on the sundeck at the bow, staring at the brown water sliding around the corners of their hull. It should have been perfect — a week's holiday on a big, flat-bottomed houseboat, exploring the river.

'Why do I feel like this?' he thought.

They had the brown river to themselves, except for the passing ghosts of paddle-steamers from an earlier age when the riverboat trade of the River Murray rivalled that of the Mississippi, with three hundred registered companies.

A breeze ruffled Matt's dark hair, cooling him. It should have been perfect, but it was the first family holiday where Matt wondered if he belonged any more. He still loved the river, its mysterious turns and its shimmering reaches and the throngs of willows and gums that lined its banks, but something had changed.

'Maybe I'm too old to be on holiday with my family any more,' he thought.

At fourteen? It couldn't be true. He felt bad about even thinking it. He felt ungrateful and disloyal about his feelings, yet he longed to be grown-up and free.

An old paddle-steamer came into view on the far side of the river. At first he thought it was stuck high and dry on the river bank, but as they drew nearer he saw that it lay marooned inside an enclosed wet dock. It was a sidewheeler with white paddle-boxes, a flat, broad hull painted in faded orange and grey, a double-storey deckhouse and a crane with two masts like insect grabs on the foredeck.

A young girl, dressed in clothes from the riverboat age, stood at the rail on the upper deck.

Matt blinked. The girl wore an old-fashioned, full-length dress that was sepia-coloured like a museum photo and it fluttered around her legs in the breeze. Her long brown hair, held back from her face in an Alice band, blew softly around her. She saw him staring and shyly waved.

Matt wondered if he should wave back. Before he could decide, a sound of tapping on the window behind him distracted him.

It was his father. There was a shine of excitement in his eyes. He'd spotted the paddlewheeler, too. He waved to Matt. Matt looked back at the paddle-steamer. The girl was gone. As quickly as that. He shrugged and went inside.

His father sat on a stool at the driving console, one hand on the wheel, the other holding a mug of coffee. Matt's mother and little sister Rebecca — 'Bexie' — sat at a coffee table playing cards.

'That's the Paddle-Steamer *Return*,' his father said. 'I've read all about her. She's a static museum now.'

Matt's father grinned at him. Matt groaned silently. His father was wearing that dumb-looking skipper's cap again, he thought. Once Matt had liked the cap. He felt it gave his father — and their river holidays — an air of racy adventure. Now it embarrassed him.

Why did his father have to wear it, especially indoors? He was no more exposed to the elements in here than if he were sitting in his living room at home, operating the TV remote control. In fact, a living room was exactly what this room was — a combined dining room and day/night lounge as the brochure described it, with a driving console area at the front window.

His father was going to give him another lecture about the bygone riverboat age, Matt thought. His father had been born in the wrong century. He would have preferred to have been a riverboat captain instead of a salesman in a big company. Perhaps that was why he'd insisted on hiring a paddlewheel houseboat for the family instead of one with a modern inboard engine or twin outboards.

'The Murray deserves to hear the beat of paddles again, Matt,' he said. 'It's the river's heartbeat.' He thought he was helping to keep the past alive.

Matt loved paddle-steamers, too. But he didn't live in the past — he longed for the future — and he felt an urge to resist his father's view of things. He wondered why he felt this way. He remembered how not long before, perhaps even on their last holiday, he would have listened enraptured as his father told him about Australia's riverboat heritage and its race of rivermen. His father had made a study of Australia's inland paddlewheelers.

'She started out life as a wool carrier, pulling barges, but she was later converted for snagging,' his father said.

He waited for Matt to ask him questions, his

alert, inquisitive blue eyes searching his son's face. He was disappointed. Matt's mind was somewhere else. Matt was thinking about the girl who had waved to him.

'Fallen red gums used to jam the Murray,' his father went on. 'Dangerous obstacles. Redgum is resistant to rotting in water and it won't float, so redgum trunks and branches lie hidden under the water like battering rams, waiting to hole the unwary boat. A redgum snag could punch a hole right through a paddleboat's four inch planks and sometimes the only clue to their presence was a few streaks and swirls on the surface of the water that looked for all the world like a platypus or a cod swimming underneath. Sinkings were common.

'That's why they had special boats dedicated to removing snags and keeping the channels free for traffic. The PS *Return* was one of them. In her time she used that deck crane and her winch to raise three million snags from the Murray. Imagine three million drowned redgum trees!'

The girl could almost have been a ghost, Matt thought. She'd vanished so suddenly. Maybe she was a reflection off the water or something he'd dreamt up, a product of his boredom and loneliness. One minute she'd been there, the next gone.

His father frowned at him. He could see that Matt wasn't listening.

Matt's mother noticed the silence that arose between them and she glanced up from her game of cards. 'Matthew, are you listening to your father? He's trying to tell you something.' She prodded him with a glare and his little sister Bexie copied her expression.

'I'm listening.'

'It was a hard life on the river,' his father continued. 'There weren't just snags to contend with, but hidden reefs and sandbanks and the danger of sparks from the stacks starting fires on board, in spite of spark-arresters. You could always tell passengers who travelled a lot on riverboats. They had cinder holes burnt in their clothing and the ladies had holes burnt in their parasols. And if fire wasn't bad enough, there'd be floods. When the Murray was aflush it could drown whole forests and turn stretches of the narrow course into treacherous lakes many kilometres wide.

'Then there were low rivers when even the shallowest draught vessels hit bottom. They'd be stranded for months at a time and the captains had to pay off their crews. Amazing what little clearance the hulls needed, though. It was said that a riverman with faith in his heart could float his riverboat on the dew.'

A smile fought with the corners of his father's mouth as if a joke were trying to find its way out. Here comes one of Dad's little made-up stories, Matt thought. Wait for it.

'Do you know how dry the river could get, Matt?'

Matt didn't really want to know, but his father was going to tell him anyway.

'One year, it was so dry that the paddlewheels kicked up dust instead of water. But a shrewd skipper found a simple way to keep his boat going. He gave his dogs big bowls of water to drink. Then he sent them running along the dry river bottom ahead of the boat. You can imagine what happened. Every now and then the dogs would stop and lift their legs. Do you know what — that's all it took to keep the boat going!'

The story delighted Matt's five-year-old sister Bexie. She giggled. 'The dogs must have had *very* big drinks of water, Daddy!'

Matt's mother chuckled.

Matt fought down a scornful laugh. Pretty dumb story, he thought. Just the sort of yarn his father loved telling.

'It was an adventurous age, but sadly it's gone. All that's left are a few river ghosts. Like that one over there,' his father said, glancing at the *Return* that was sliding by their port side.

'Yes, but it had to end,' Matt said, challenging his father's point of view. 'Just imagine what the river would be like today if riverboats and their barges were still swarming all over it.'

'Wonderful,' his father said.

'Yes, but you wouldn't be able to have a lazy time like this on the river. It'd be like travelling on a freeway with semi-trailers all around you. And think of the environment. The riverboatmen would have cut down the redgums to burn in their furnaces. And we'd have more pollution! You can't live in the past. You've got to look ahead.'

His father was surprised by the force of his son's argument. He couldn't argue with Matt's logic, but there was a slap in it and his father felt it. He put down his coffee mug. He accidentally spilt a drop over the brim. It hit the carpeted floor like a brown tear. 'Is that really what you think, Matt? Or are you just being otherwise, the way you prefer to be these days?'

Matt's mother gave Matt a pleading look. 'I don't know what's got into you, Matt,' she said despairingly. 'You never used to be like this when you were younger. Please. Can't everything just be nice?'

'Yes, but I'm allowed to have a point of view, aren't I?' His mother had a favourite saying when life was pleasant and things were going smoothly: *'It's nice when everything's nice.'* She always wanted things to be 'nice', especially for Matt's father. She hadn't said it a lot lately.

Matt wished everything could be nice. But it didn't *feel* nice. He felt trapped. He was tired of going along with his father's point of view. He was tired of being stuck on the houseboat with his family. It was as if he'd been asked to put his life on hold and time were standing still. What were his friends back home doing? He burnt with impatience. He wanted to get on with his life.

'I don't think people should keep looking back,' he said defensively. 'We've got to face the future.'

'The future comes all too soon,' his father said, frowning. 'Don't be in too much of a rush to join it.'

Matt went back onto the sundeck.

They didn't understand. They thought he was being awkward. They'd be happier if he were a small kid again, he thought. If they could turn back his life like a clock, they would do it. They wanted things to be the way they used to be before he had his own ideas and dreams, before he seemed so sure of himself. If only they knew. He wasn't nearly so sure of himself as he seemed. A part of him still wanted to feel the way he used to feel.

Maybe I was happier then, when I was a little kid, he thought. I'm certainly not very happy now.

He looked down at the current. Pity you couldn't go against the flow of time. If this was what it felt like growing up, it wasn't much fun.

2

The PS Return

THEY MOORED SHORTLY AFTERWARDS in the deep shade of willow trees near a river town. His mother and sister wanted to go shopping in the town and his father wanted to visit a local bank.

'Why don't you come with me and then we'll take a look at the *Return* on the way back?' his father said.

'Um, no, I feel like hanging around, thanks.'

His mother gave Matt a prompting glare. 'You've been moping around, looking cooped up all day. Here's your chance to get out.'

Matt wanted to visit the paddle-steamer, but not with his father, at least not straightaway. He wanted some time there alone. He was still wondering about the girl.

'Suit yourself, Matt,' his father said, shrugging.

'Go along with your father, Matt,' his mother

said in a weary tone.

'Perhaps Matt isn't interested in seeing the paddleboat,' his father said.

'No, I am, really. I'd like to see it.'

'But not with me.'

'I didn't say that. I just thought I'd like to go straight there. I'll go ahead and meet you there.'

His father brightened.

'Fair enough, Matt. But wait for me. Don't go steaming off anywhere.'

Bexie shook her head at her father. 'Silly Daddy. The paddleboat can't go anywhere. It's stuck in a lock.'

'Not a lock, sweetheart. Locks are enclosed chambers with gates on each end that vessels have to go through. They raise or lower vessels from one river level to another.'

'I mean it's locked *in*.'

'I know what you mean, Bexie,' Matt's father said affectionately. He scooped up his daughter and carried her down the gangplank to the river bank.

Matt remembered when his father used to do that with him. He saw a memory of it in his mind like a piece of moving film. He saw himself being hoisted clear of the ground by his father's big hands and felt again the secure feeling of being swung through the air and the pleasant bump of his father's step as he walked along with him. That was a long, long time ago.

Bexie loved it and giggled.

Matt walked along the river bank under stooped willows, kicking stones with the toe of his sneaker. He joined a road that ran parallel with the river, and quickened his pace. He thought of the girl who had waved to him from the paddlewheeler. A girl of his own age. The thought lifted his spirits.

The road curved, climbed. He followed it round and down and there it was, nestled in its enclosed dock on the river bank.

The PS *Return*. The old paddle-steamer sat dreaming in the late afternoon sunshine, surrounded by lawn and a protective wire fence.

A yellow board told the story of the *Return*. His eye picked out a few details. . .

The PS Return *was constructed in 1911 at Goolwa, South Australia. . . she was composite built with jarrah planking and kauri deck. . . 2 cylinder 30hp steam engines built by boiler-makers in Gawler. . . the cylinders are 366 mm in diameter and have a 762 ml stroke. . . one of the few original constructions not burnt to the waterline and rebuilt like many others. . . she kept the river open for traffic by removing snags and was later used in the construction of locks. . .*

The area was deserted. Was the floating museum still open? It was getting late. He pushed a turnstile in the fence and went inside. A path led to the vessel's gangplank. He followed it, looking up at the paddlewheeler. It reminded him of his grandmother's tiny white fibro cottage in Sydney, except this one was fixed onto a hull. He warmed to it.

He almost bumped into a metal box mounted on a post beside the path. A small sign on it said:

The Friends of the PS Return *invite you to make a donation for the restoration of this historic vessel.*

Invite you to make a donation, he noted. That meant he didn't have to. All the same, he felt like doing it. She was beautiful and his heart went out to her. Perhaps his father was right. You had to keep the past alive. He dug into his jeans pockets and came up with a single coin.

Not much, in fact the last of his pocket money. Too bad it wasn't more. He dropped it into the box.

As he went on he noticed that the box was open at the back. No padlock. Trusting people, he thought. Anyone could take the money.

He saw a pink smudge of movement at a window on the deckhouse and looked up quickly.

Nothing.

Matt went up the gangplank, run out beside one of the big white paddle-boxes, and found himself on the reddish timber planking of a broad main deck. He'd visit the upper deck first. That was where the girl had been. He took a companionway to the top level and went along the narrow, verandah-like deck. He came to a door and tried it. It opened and he stepped into a large saloon. There was a table in the saloon, some chairs and some yellowing photographs in frames on the walls, mostly of whiskered former skippers.

Their eyes glared at him from their photographs, making him feel like an invader. He saw some board games jammed in a shelf — Trivial Pursuit, Scrabble and some others. No girl in here. Just ghosts.

Then a hand tapped him on the shoulder.

'Boo!'

Matt, already seized with a feeling of guilt, gave a gasp. He twisted. A lanky boy about his own age, with a blond fringe of hair and teasing eyes, laughed at him.

'Got you! You thought I was a ghost. I scared you to absolute death. I think.'

'Thanks a lot,' Matt said, smiling in relief in spite of himself. The kid had an outrageous grin and the world's worst haircut.

'Who are you?'

Matt introduced himself.

'You live around here?'

'I'm on holiday. We're here on a houseboat.'

'Who's we?'

'My parents and sister.' Matt parted reluctantly with the information.

'Yeah, I'm here with my oldies, too,' the boy said. 'We're camped at the caravan park. I really hate it — a bit. I'm Jamie. Have you seen the engine yet?' Matt shook his head. 'Then come and check it out, but bring your money with you.' Matt wondered what the boy meant, but followed him. Jamie bounded down the companionway, making the timbers creak.

They returned to the main deck and went down another metal companionway into an engine pit where they could see the great bulk of the steam engine with its boiler and flywheel and pistons sticking out like shiny iron arms bared from their sleeves. It had the hot smell of grease and working metal. The stranger pointed to what looked like another donation box.

'You can start the engines. Look.'

A sign read:

Insert coin in box to turn paddlewheels. The PS Return's paddlewheels and engine components can be motivated by coin operation, giving a realistic impression of the vessel's mechanics.

'Pity,' Matt said disappointedly.

'What's a pity?'

'I don't have any money. Do you have any?'

'Not much. Not a cent.'

'I put my last coin in the donation box outside,' Matt said. It would have been great to fire up the engine. Now he was paying for his stupid little act of generosity.

'The donation box isn't locked,' Jamie told him, a mischievous gleam in his eyes. 'You can easily get your money back.'

'That would be stealing.'

'Garbage. It's your money and it was a donation, so you didn't have to give it. Anyway, you're not going to keep it. You're going to put it in this engine.'

'Yes, but the money I gave was for the restoration fund. If I spend it here, it's for my own fun.'

'Garbage. It's all the same to them. If you won't get it, I will. Stay here, I'll get it back for you.'

'I don't think—'

His impulsive new friend climbed out of the engine pit back onto the deck and disappeared from view down the gangplank.

This isn't right, Matt thought. But he was eager to wake up the sleeping mass of steel. The engine reeked of latent power. His father would be along soon. He'd replace the money he'd taken back. How did a single coin set it off? he wondered. Probably electrics. He peered into the slot at the top of the coin box.

'I waved at you when you went by on your houseboat,' a young girl's voice said. 'Why didn't you wave back?'

He looked up. He wasn't going to be startled a second time. Where had she sprung from?

She stood at the edge of the engine pit, looking down at him with a gentle smile on her face. It was the old-fashioned girl in the long dress and with the soft billowing hair flowing from under an Alice band. The girl had a dreamy face and a grave-eyed stare that expected an explanation from him.

'I wanted to wave back but something distracted me,' Matt said. The excuse sounded feeble now.

Who was she? Why was she dressed like this? It was a bit eerie seeing somebody dressed in clothes from a bygone age aboard an old paddleboat. Was she trying to scare people? She probably enjoyed creeping up on them and giving them a good fright, he thought.

He couldn't help staring at her costume. She could have stepped out of a museum. She even wore laced-up granny boots with boot buttons. 'Why are you dressed like that?' he asked.

'Lots of people dress like this. The friends of the *Return* dress like this on the weekends to add to the historical atmosphere. The friends serve Devonshire teas to raise money.'

'Are you a friend?' he said.

'I could be,' she replied, twisting his meaning. 'Are you looking for one? You seemed so sad and lonely standing on the deck of your houseboat.'

Matt coloured a little. 'I mean are you a friend of the *Return*?'

'It would be hard not to be a friend of such a lovely old boat. Would you like scones and tea? I can make you some, if you like. It's all sitting there in the galley.'

'I haven't got any money,' he was going to say, then he felt a twinge of guilt. What would she think if she learnt that he was out of money and that Jamie had gone to get back his coin? He changed it to a simple, 'No thanks.'

'What's your name?' she said.

'Matt.'

'I'm Emma Jane.'

It had an old-fashioned ring to Matt's ears, like the name of a riverboat. He heard the clump of Jamie's feet coming back on deck.

'Hi,' Jamie said cheerily.

'This is Emma Jane,' Matt said to the face that peered down. 'One of the friends of the *Return.*'

'Oh, hi Emma. I'm Jamie. We're about to start up the engine.'

He climbed down the iron-runged companionway to join Matt in the engine pit. 'Here,' he said, handing the coin hastily to Matt as if it were burning his palm. 'I really think you should have the fun of starting it. I suppose.'

'Be careful,' the girl said. 'Put that coin in there and start the engine and who knows where the *Return* will take you. Maybe she will take you back into the past.'

'Maybe that'd be good,' Matt said, remembering his argument with his father. 'Some people would prefer me to be back in the past.'

'They want you to go back? Why?'

'Going back would be absolutely wild,' Jamie said. 'I think.'

Matt took the money between two fingers and held it over the slot in the coin box. He hesitated. The coin flared in a beam of afternoon sun that found its way into the engine pit.

'Put that coin in there and start the engine and who knows where the Return will take you. Maybe she will take you back into the past.'

'Maybe that'd be good. Some people would prefer me to be back in the past.'

The words rang in his ears. Time stopped for Matt. It hung there like the coin in his fingers:

'They want you to go back? Why?'

He glanced at Jamie and saw that his eyes were alight, like the shining of coins. He looked at the girl. Her fingers had clenched around the rail that ran around the engine pit. The fingers were whitening.

Matt's own fingers locked, wouldn't part. Let go. Fall. The fingers opened with a reluctant twitch. He let go and the coin dropped. It dropped for an age. He heard the far-off metallic clink as it hit the bottom of the iron box. It echoed in the engine pit and the echo stretched to eternity.

3

The past awakened

THE *RETURN'S* STEAM ENGINE awoke from its slumber.

The big flywheel spun and the pistons flashed and pumped like a heart driving life to the paddle-shafts. They heard a rumble and a slow *plash, plash, plash* as the paddles began to turn.

'Let's go up and watch,' Jamie shouted.

The beat of the paddles grew like approaching thunder as the paddles thrashed the water. Very realistic. Too realistic. Was it just the clamour of the engine working that gave Matt the sudden shocking sensation of movement? Or were they actually going backwards?

Three sharp blasts of a steam whistle cracked across their heads like whiplashes.

Alarm jumped into Emma Jane's eyes. She stared at the upper deck above her as if she could see right through the planking. There were tearing and squealing sounds. The paddlewheeler was going astern, thrashing against her enclosure like a great cod in a net.

'Who blew the whistle?' Matt said to the girl.

Emma Jane shook her head. She was pale.

Jamie swarmed up the iron companionway to the main deck. With a screech the gangplank scraped off the deck and fell away into the water with a splash.

'Is this supposed to be happening?' Matt shouted.

'No,' the girl shouted back.

'Then tell us what's going on!'

'Somebody's taking us into the river.'

'Who?'

'I don't know.'

Jamie was already running to the upper deck to see. Matt left the engine pit and followed. On the upper deck they looked over the side. The *Return*'s paddles were throwing white water from her paddle-boxes and the entire boat strained and squealed and shuddered, a bound Titan throwing off its ropes.

The two boys reached the wheelhouse and peered in through the glass. A man wearing a skipper's cap reached out for the telegraph handle and moved it from 'half' to 'full speed astern'. *Cling!* Then he gripped the wheel.

Jamie rapped on the glass. Maybe the man didn't know they were on board. It was some mistake. Matt joined Jamie, tapping on the glass. The man ignored them and adjusted the big wooden wheel. The paddlewheeler was throwing itself around like a bucking horse.

Matt felt a dank fear slide down his collar. 'He won't listen.'

'This is amazing. I reckon,' Jamie said.

They tried to enter the wheelhouse but the doors were locked on the inside. Matt rapped on the glass again.

The man turned to look at him. He had alert, inquisitive blue eyes that searched Matt's face. A smile fought with the corners of his mouth as if a joke were trying to find its way out.

'You've got to let us off!' Matt shouted.

The man shook his head. Matt saw him mouth the words: 'We're going back.'

Back? Where?

They were going backwards, that was for sure. Matt almost toppled. With a final wrench and a shrieking sound, the structure of wire and poles that formed the rear of the wet dock gave way and the paddle-steamer churned into the river.

Now the man grabbed the telegraph again, this time stopping the paddles. *Cling. Cling. Cling. Cling.* They drifted back into the river.

Now he rammed the telegraph to 'full steam ahead'. Matt heard another series of *clings*.

The paddles churned. 'What do we do?' Jamie said. 'We've got to jump. I think.'

'And leave Emma? We can't. Somebody will see what's happening. You can't hide a boat like this on the river. Somebody will come after us and stop him.'

'You're right. Of course they will. I hope.'

They were out in the middle of the river now. The paddlewheeler was moving forward, taking them upstream.

'You've got to let us off,' Matt yelled at the man in the wheelhouse. Was he deaf? Or crazy? Or both? He stood as motionless as a wooden carving in the wheelhouse.

Matt and Jamie tore themselves reluctantly away from the wheelhouse and went to look for Emma.

'I'm positive she's jumped. I reckon,' Jamie said. But when they ran around the lower deck looking over the side there was no sign of her.

'What now?'

'Check the berths.'

The first berth behind the wheelhouse, marked 'captain', had a locked door, but all the rest opened. They tried the other side of the deckhouse. There was no trace of the girl.

They went down the companionway and

Matt found her in a small galley. She was buttering some scones on a plate.

'Do you want some tea?' she said, looking up. 'Don't look so worried. I won't charge you.'

Didn't she care about what was happening to them, Matt wondered. Emma Jane was in a world of her own, happily at work in the galley. The homely sight of her buttering the scones had a peculiarly calming effect on him. It seemed to stop the action or at least slow things down, made the crazy events that were unfolding seem unreal, as if he had switched off an exciting episode on television to break for afternoon tea.

Perhaps she expected this to happen. Was it all part of the show? Maybe this happened every day of the week to entertain the tourists.

Then he remembered the shrieking sound as the wire and poles that formed the rear of the wet dock had given way, remembered how the gangplank had fallen into the water. With a sinking feeling he hoped was purely mental, Matt realised this wasn't part of the show.

Jamie squeezed into the galley behind him. They both stared open-mouthed at the girl. She took a muslin lid off a jar of strawberry jam and spooned the shiny red contents onto the scones. 'Cream?' She pointed to a jug of freshly whipped cream. 'Help yourself.'

'You're calmly making scones in here while we're being hijacked by a raving lunatic!'

'The guy up there is totally nuts. I think,' Jamie said. 'He wouldn't even listen to us.'

'He's not a raving lunatic,' she said with certainty. 'He gave three toots on the whistle before reversing into the river, the proper procedure. That tells me he knows what he's doing. And he's handling her perfectly, even better than my father could have done. We're in good hands, so let's just relax.'

'Yes, but what's happening to us?' Matt said.

'We're going for a ride and there's nothing we can do about it. Are you going to eat one of these scones or do I have to waste them?'

She held out the plate.

'I can't eat scones now. Just one,' Jamie said, helping himself to the biggest one and spooning a healthy dollop of cream on top of the jam.

'You, Matt?'

'This is mad.'

'Is it? Maybe we really are going back in time. Isn't it what you wanted? Maybe that'd be good, you said. Some people would prefer you to be back in the past. Who was it who wanted you back in the past?'

'My father mostly.'

'My father was the same.'

Was? The question mark dangled in Matt's mind.

'But let's not worry about that now. Instead of panicking, let's think of this as an unexpected holiday surprise. You don't often get a free paddle-steamer ride, do you?'

Jamie scoffed down his scone and grabbed another. 'I'm so upset I can't eat. Not much.'

Matt accepted a scone and looked at it. It smelt good, like his mother's baking. He found himself eating it and enjoying it.

'Nice?' Emma Jane smiled.

'Great.'

'It's nice when scones are nice,' she said.

She made them some tea in mugs, sweetened with brown sugar.

'Seriously, what are we going to do?' Matt said. 'I mean what if he keeps on going with us on board? Where's he taking us? When is he going to stop? It's going to be dark soon.'

She shrugged. 'Maybe we're having a night cruise as well as an afternoon cruise. Isn't that fun?'

'Aren't you worried?' For a dreamy-looking girl she was surprisingly adventurous. Reckless maybe.

'I've decided not to be.'

Matt found himself letting go. What did he care? Things were out of his hands. Maybe

he'd just go along with it. The man was playing some practical joke. It was no time for him
to lose his sense of humour over it. He had
nothing better to do. His parents might worry,
but a break from him might make them happy.
They were sick of him.

'Please help me wash up,' Emma Jane said.

'You want us to help?' Jamie said, moving to
the door.

'Back here,' she said firmly. 'Of course I
want you to help. I'll wash, you two can dry.'
She gave them teatowels and made them do it.

Afterwards they went out on deck. The
throngs of willows were gathering density in
the growing dark.

They were travelling into a deepening
mystery, Matt thought.

4

Playing games

THEY SAT ON THE DECK with their backs against the deckhouse. Matt was in a world of numb reflection, listening to the thunder of the paddles. The boat had carried them off, shaken off its imprisonment in the wet dock and hijacked them upriver. It couldn't happen, but it had.

The stolen coin. He should never have let Jamie steal it. That was it. He was being punished. He should never have dropped it into the coin box. If only he could get it back. If only he could *go* back.

Perhaps he was going back. That's what Emma Jane had said. He looked at the gentle profile of the girl beside him. Strange, placid, dreamy girl. Nothing seemed to bother her. She had the patience of another age, like the strong patience his grandmother had always displayed. He noticed holes in her dress.

Then he remembered what his father had told him:

'There weren't just snags to contend with, but. . . the danger of sparks from the stacks starting fires on board, in spite of spark-arresters. You could always tell passengers who travelled a lot on riverboats. They'd have cinder holes burnt in their clothing and the ladies had holes burnt in their parasols. . .'

'Look,' Emma Jane said, before he could ask her about it.

The paddlewheeler had turned on two powerful headlamps, like yellow eyes. The beams reached to a bend in the river and the light threw up a stand of ghost gum trees.

'Maybe we should try to reason with him again,' Matt suggested. 'Or ask him to let us in on the joke.'

'If you like,' Emma Jane said. 'But I don't think it will do much good.'

They went to the upper deck and gathered at the side of the wheelhouse. The silhouette of the skipper looked like a cut-out in the darkness. They could see beams of the headlamps invading the passing river banks.

Together, they tapped energetically on the glass, but the captain kept his eyes fixed ahead.

The profile was familiar, Matt thought. The man looked quite a lot like his father.

'I thought it would be a waste of time,' Emma Jane said.

'I don't understand how this boat is going,' said Matt. 'Who's stoking up the furnace? What's making us go?'

'You put a coin in the slot didn't you?' queried Emma Jane.

Matt and Jamie exchanged guilty glances.

'We might as well pass the time enjoying ourselves,' Emma Jane suggested. She took them to the large saloon at the rear of the upper deckhouse. 'This used to be the officer's dining saloon,' she said. 'The *Return* had a whole crew living on board — the master, engineer and fireman — as well as two or three deckhands. The master's wife and daughter would also take trips with them.'

She turned on some electric lights, powered by a generator somewhere. 'You can see them in these faded photographs all around us.' She went to the shelf where the stack of games was kept. 'There are some board games here. Lots of children have played in this room over the years. In fact, we call it the games saloon now. What game shall we play?' She dug into a cupboard. 'Cards, Trivial Pursuit, Scrabble? That's all we've got, except tiddlywinks.'

'What's tiddlywinks?' Both boys looked blank.

'It's a very old game. It's a board game with a cup in the middle and lots of little flat coloured counters called tiddlywinks. You make the tiddlywinks jump into the cup by pressing down the edge of them with a larger counter and flicking them. It's a game for small children. . .'

'You wouldn't catch me playing a childish game like that,' Matt thought.

'Got any computer games?' Jamie said.

Now it was Emma Jane's turn to look blank. 'I don't know about those.'

'You must know about computer games,' Matt said.

'She's kidding. I think,' Jamie agreed.

'No I'm not. Anyway you two don't know about tiddlywinks. So don't be so superior.'

The two boys looked at each other in puzzlement. They settled for Trivial Pursuit.

'I'd better warn you,' Jamie said at the outset. 'I'm a whizz at Trivial Pursuit. I always win. Almost.'

Matt wondered whether he meant that he almost always won or that he always *almost* won. There was a difference. But it was hard to know with Jamie, who seemed to be in two minds about everything.

'You're not very sure of what you say, are you?'
Matt said, growing irritated by the boy's habit of
going into reverse on everything he'd said.

'Are *you* sure of things, Matt?' asked Emma
Jane.

'Some things.'

'Like going back? You said it would be a
good thing. Did you really think so?'

'Why not?' he said recklessly.

They could hear the steady *boof boof boof* of
the paddles, the long twisting shudders that ran
the length of the vessel and the panting of the
exhaust as they began to play.

There was something strange about this
game, Matt soon discovered. It was like no
other game of Trivial Pursuit he had ever
played. All the questions were about the river.
He landed on green. Science and nature.

'What introduced species has actually helped
preserve the River Murray?' Emma Jane asked.

'The Murray River cod,' Jamie said firmly.
'Definitely, or is it the European carp? No,
wrong again, they're killing off the cod.'

Emma Jane read the answer from her card.
'The willow tree.' She put the card back in the
box and explained. 'If it weren't for the willows, with their strong root systems, the banks
would be washed away by the wakes of boats.'

Matt thought of all the pleasure boats and

skiers who used the river as a playground. It made sense.

'I knew that,' Jamie said.

It was Matt's turn. He threw the dice and landed on yellow — history.

'What did the Aborigines call the stern-wheeler boats?'

Matt knew this one. He remembered his father telling him about it — in the days when he used to listen to his father's stories.

'The Aborigines called stern-wheeler boats wheelbarrow boats,' Matt said.

'Right.' Emma Jane rewarded him with a smile of congratulation.

'Wheelbarrow. I get it,' Jamie said. 'Or do I?'

'Wheelbarrows have one wheel in the front,' Matt explained. 'And stern-wheelers have one wheel at the back. So they looked a bit like wheelbarrows going backwards.'

'Then why didn't the Aborigines call them backward wheelbarrows?'

'You're backward,' Matt said. 'I thought you were good at Trivial Pursuit.'

'I told you. I almost win all the time. But I never actually do.'

It was Emma's turn. She landed on brown — art and literature. Matt drew a card and asked a question. 'Who described the old river-boatmen as looking more like drovers than sailors and the crews as being very much like the unemployed?'

'Henry Lawson.'

Geography was next.

'How long is the Murray from its source?' Three choices: 2 600, 2 200 or 1 900 kilometres. 2 600 was the closest answer. And so the game went on.

Emma Jane won easily and Matt was surprised to be beaten. He felt unreasonably disappointed.

'Another game,' he suggested.

She won that too. He wished he'd listened harder to his father's stories. Losing a second time didn't make it any easier. He was even more disappointed.

'What about tiddlywinks?' he said, surprising himself.

Emma gave him a flicker of a frown. 'I told you tiddlywinks was for small children.'

'I've got to beat you at something.'

'One more game of this, then,' she said. They played Trivial Pursuit again and Emma won a third game.

'Then it's definitely tiddlywinks time,' said Matt. Suddenly he felt eager to play the game. It didn't sound so silly any more.

'Not tonight,' she said. 'It's late.'

As if he agreed with her, Jamie yawned.

'Let's go out onto the deck and see what's happening,' he said. 'It's getting past my beddy-byes.' He sounded like a six-year-old, Matt thought.

Emma put the games away tidily and they went out. It was a velvety night, sparked with stars, and the paddlewheeler's funnel belched another firmament of cloud and stars over their heads. The sparks flew up from her stack into the night and quickly died. The paddle-wheeler's big headlamps made a milky highway of the river ahead and lit the silent gums. Grey water curled around their bow.

'Why don't we pick ourselves berths and get some sleep,' Emma Jane suggested. 'There's no point sitting up all night.'

'What about a quick game of tiddlywinks?' Matt persisted.

'No,' Emma Jane said firmly. 'Bed for you.'

'Aah,' Matt said, peeved, like a small kid who'd been sent to bed early. He wanted to play on.

He felt as if something heavy had slipped from his shoulders that afternoon, as if his cares were drifting away from him like the wake from their paddlewheels. He felt strangely younger — free and careless. It didn't seem to matter what was happening to him any more. It was all a game and an adventure. It was fun.

'Nightey-night,' he said to Emma Jane.

Jamie yawned. 'I've never been so tired in my life. Hardly ever.'

'Good night boys,' Emma Jane said.

They each chose a berth on the upper deck. The cabins were little bigger than telephone booths inside, Matt discovered. He closed the door of his berth and fell on the bunk, still fully dressed. The cabin smelled a bit damp and mildewy, like the inside of his grandmother's fibro cottage in Sydney. That comforted him.

The mattress was hard and thin, but he didn't care. He sank into the arms of sleep, listening to the throb of the paddlewheeler and feeling the boat's wooden sinews flexing. It reminded Matt of being small again and being scooped up and carried by his father. He felt himself being lifted clear of his cares, felt the snug feeling of letting go and knowing he was safe. The bump of the paddles was a bit like the pleasant bump of his father's step as he walked along with him. He smiled in his sleep.

It wasn't such a long time ago, really.

It was funny about the skipper looking a bit like his father. His father would have loved to have been a riverboat captain instead of sales-man for a big company. He had been born in the wrong century. Perhaps his father had been right to look backwards. There was nothing wrong with living in the past, not if it felt like this. The past was snug and safe. It was the future that was scary: the unknown.

Matt didn't long for it any more. The future didn't seem important. He was content. Life was much simpler when you were little, before you wanted to follow your own ideas and dreams. It was much easier to rely on others and to go along with their opinions and ideas.

He felt himself letting go of his own ideas and dreams as he drifted into sleep. Don't try to take control. Leave it to others. Give in to stronger forces around you, like this churning riverboat that is carrying you away. Don't take steps into the unknown. Go along for the ride and enjoy yourself. The future is out of your hands.

Matt drifted towards sleep and into a feeling of freedom. Cares slipped away from him. He pictured the wake of the paddleboat fanning out behind them, rippling out across the river and gently lapping against the river bank. It was the past, spread out clearly to see.

He pictured the twin headlamps out front searching the mysterious depths of the forest, probing the unknown. He saw shining eyes in the forest and pale ghost gum trees that stood with their arms thrown up in arrested fright.

The river behind them was much safer. . .

Sleep, when it came, seemed endless.

5

The skipper

MATT WOKE UP THINKING he was back on the
family houseboat with his mother and father
and little sister Bexie.

Then he remembered where he was and a
grin rose to his face like a sun coming up. It
was the sort of dawning delight he used to feel
as a little boy when he woke up to remember
it was Christmas morning or Easter egg day.

He was on a paddlewheeler on a magical
adventure. Morning light streamed through a
glass panel in the door. Suddenly, he realised
the paddles had stopped. All was quiet.
Where were they?

He rolled off his bunk, yawned, and
stretched his arms in the air. His jeans fell
down around his ankles. He quickly yanked
them up. Funny. His belt must have come
undone in the night. He looked down at the belt.

No, it was still firmly secured. Why was it loose? He slid a hand behind the belt and held it out from his stomach. You could get two of me in here, he thought. Maybe it was because he had missed supper. He felt hollow inside.

Matt undid the buckle and drew the belt tighter, fastening it again. His shirt ballooned baggily around him. He tucked the loose ends into his jeans.

But he still wasn't right. Matt took a step and almost fell over. He was standing on the legs of his jeans and they were tripping him up. Why were they suddenly so long? Are these *my* jeans? They looked big enough to be his father's.

Matt wondered what to do. Roll up the legs I suppose, he decided. He bent and rolled up the legs, giving them two big turns. Then he noticed his sneakers. They looked as big as boats. He tightened the laces. It helped, but only a bit.

I'd better eat soon before I shrink away completely, he thought.

There was a small mirror sitting on a ledge in the berth. Perhaps he'd better have a look at himself. Matt stood on tiptoes and took the mirror down. He gazed into the silvery surface. His eyes swam in the reflection. Good. The sight reassured him. He looked pretty big in there. Unless. . .

He flipped it over. It was a double-sided shaving mirror. He'd been looking at the side with magnification. Now he'd shrunk. The reflection on the other side shocked him. A little boy with frightened eyes stared out of the mirror at him.

Matt almost dropped the mirror in fright.

He flipped it back to the magnified side. This was better. Maybe it was just the contrast of going from magnification strength to normal that made him appear to change and look younger. He flipped it back to the normal side. He made a face at himself. A cheeky eight-year-old in the mirror copied his expression. This was weird. He went back to the magnification. This must be the way I really look, he thought. Maybe it's one of those trick mirrors that you see at fun shows. Maybe somebody has put it in here to play a trick on me.

Still, it had given him a jolt and he didn't fancy looking at himself in the normal side again.

He put the mirror back on the shelf. Breakfast would put things right. He remembered his mother's advice: 'If you want to grow up big one day, you have to eat a good breakfast.'

Matt opened the door. A beautiful yellow

sun made him blink. It was like the sunny yolk of a boiled egg at breakfast time. He remembered breakfast times as a small boy. He pictured a little red eggcup he used to have. It was made of pottery and fashioned in the shape of an Easter rabbit. It had come with a little Easter egg inside it. Whatever had happened to it? He hadn't seen it for years. It would be fun to eat out of it again, just for old time's sake.

He went out onto the deck, stretching and yawning. Where were the others?

The *Return* was at anchor in the river, near some willows. Why had they stopped here? Matt went to the wheelhouse to look for the skipper, but the wheelhouse was empty. Had he gone ashore? Where had he brought them? Who cared! It was a beautiful day.

He'd find the others. Maybe they were in the games room already, having fun without him. He was filled with suspicion. He went to the games saloon, opened the door and peered inside. Empty. The boxes of games were still sitting on the shelf where Emma Jane had put them. Good. The others must still be asleep. Should he wake them? No, this was a good chance to have some fun without them. His eye settled on the tiddlywinks box.

He took it down from the shelf and opened it up on the table. It had a little red cup in the centre of the playing board — like the eggcup he remembered. The game had plastic discs like flat Smarties, he noticed. He recalled Emma Jane's description of the game:

'It's a very old game. It's a board game with a cup in the middle and lots of little flat coloured counters called tiddlywinks. You make the tiddlywinks jump into the cup by pressing down the edge of them with a larger counter and flicking them. It's a game for small children. . .'

He saw it now. You held one of the bigger plastic counters in your fingers and pressed down on the edge of a tiddlywink and it would spring into the air. The point of the game was to land it inside the red cup.

Matt took the board off the table and spread it on the floor of the games saloon, crouching on his knees over it. He pressed a yellow counter with a bigger one. It clicked, flicked up and landed with a satisfying rattle in the cup. Goal! He tried a few more. He kept missing. You had to concentrate. It was tricky. He found his tongue creeping into the corner of his mouth as he played. He chose a green counter. This one would go in. He was about to give it a firm click, when a pair of big shoes stepped into the circle of his vision.

He gulped.

'It's good to see you having fun, son.'

He looked up at the towering figure of a man. The man's bright, alert eyes under his skipper's cap looked down at him fondly. The skipper didn't look very scary now. He looked quite friendly, even more like Matt's father.

The skipper fought down a smile that tried to escape from the corners of his mouth. 'Do you know I thought we had crickets in here with all this clicking going on. Woke me up. What a racket.'

'Sorry,' Matt said.

'Only joking.' The man sank into a chair that creaked under his body. 'You go ahead and play. I'll just watch you.'

Matt shrugged. He clicked a red counter into the cup. Another point. He hoped the skipper had noticed. The skipper clapped his big hands and Matt glowed. He popped two more into the cup just to show him.

'Don't you want to know where we are?' the skipper asked.

'No,' Matt said, lining up a yellow counter to shoot at the cup.

'Aren't you worried?'

'No, I'm playing now.'

'It must be fine to be young again,' the skipper said.

Matt wondered what he meant. He supposed he meant it would be fine for the skipper if he could be young again. He plinked the yellow counter into the cup. It was getting fuller now, but there were still a few to go.

'Don't you miss anything?' the skipper said.

'I've missed quite a few, don't worry.'

'No, I mean about being older.'

'You miss things, do you?' Matt said.

'No, not me. This is fine really. It's just what I wanted. I mean you. Do you miss things?'

'I miss a red eggcup I used to have. Don't know what happened to it. I thought about it this morning. It was shaped like an Easter bunny. It came with a real Easter egg inside the eggcup.'

A frown drew lines in the captain's face. 'But tell me. Weren't there things you were looking forward to?'

Matt paused to think about it. 'Yes. I was looking forward to breakfast. May I have a boiled egg, please?'

'No, I mean about growing up.'

'When I grow up I'd like to be a riverboat captain like you.'

The captain gave a sad smile. 'I'm afraid there might not be riverboats when you grow up. The riverboat age has to end. Just imagine what the river would be like in the future if riverboats and their barges kept swarming all over it.'

'Wonderful,' Matt said.

'Yes, but you wouldn't be able to have a lazy time on the river. It'd be like travelling on a freeway with semi-trailers all around you. And think of the environment. The riverboatmen would have cut down the redgums to burn in their furnaces. And we'd have more pollution! You can't live in the past. You've got to look ahead, I suppose. When I look ahead for you I see so many exciting things, things that a father should share with you — growing up, being a friend instead of just a child, starting a career, getting married and creating a new, bigger family that everyone can enjoy. But all that won't happen now. Perhaps I haven't really thought enough about your future, Matt.'

'You know my name.'

'Of course.'

'What are we going to do then?' Matt said.

'It's too late to do anything. It's happened now. I've got what I wanted.'

Matt was crestfallen. 'I hope it isn't too late,' he said.

'It is.'

'I'm so hungry.'

'For the future?'

'For breakfast.'

'I suddenly understand that I've been incredibly selfish. I'm sorry, Matt.'

'That's all right. But I think I could eat two eggs now.'

'I wanted to keep things the way they were. But you can't keep your loved ones in a time capsule. I suppose I made you feel bad about growing up. Why did I do it? My parents didn't make me feel bad about growing up. They couldn't wait! Will you forgive me?'

Matt was starting to frown. What *was* the skipper talking about?

The man's eyes turned sad and watery as he stared at a spot on the floor. He swallowed. 'So sorry, Matthew.' He hid his face in his hands and his shoulders shook as he sobbed quietly.

'I've gone and upset him,' Matt thought. He jumped up and patted the man on the shoulder.

'Don't be upset,' he said. 'I can make my own breakfast. I'm a big boy now.'

That made things worse. Matt heard the man crying out loud. 'I've got to try to turn things around,' the skipper said with a sigh of despair.

It was best to leave him alone, Matt decided, so he skipped along the deck to the galley.

Emma Jane and Jamie were already there ahead of him. Emma Jane was cutting up scones and Jamie was goggling at them, kicking the wall annoyingly with his sneaker while he waited. Jamie's clothes looked baggy, too. He'd rolled up his pants, but his shirt billowed around him. Matt looked at Emma Jane. She looked the same as she'd looked yesterday. Perhaps she had eaten more scones than they had.

'Hi, Matt. Where've you been?' Emma Jane said.

'I've been practising tiddlywinks.'

'Aw, without me. I absolutely hate you. A bit,' Jamie said.

Matt put in his order to Emma Jane. 'I'd like two boiled eggs, please,' he said. 'The captain said I could have them.'

Emma Jane looked up. 'So the captain's out and about, is he?'

'Who cares about him?' Jamie said. 'Hurry up with the scones, Emma. Can I have Vegemite on mine?' The blond boy with the fringe kicked the wall harder in his impatience.

'Stop being childish,' she told him.

'Oh, you're so grown-up, aren't you?' Jamie said bitterly. 'You're so much bigger than me. You think.'

'Girls are older than boys,' she said.

'They can't always be older. They're only older if they're older.'

'Older in the head,' Emma Jane explained.

'More sensible.'

'You think you're a little mother, don't you?'

'No, I don't. Because I haven't got any kids except you two to look after.'

'Do you want to be a mother when you grow up?' Matt said.

'I can't see myself as a grown-up,' she said. Her eyes were big and earnest.

It was a mysterious statement. Did she mean she couldn't picture herself as a grown-up? Or did she mean she feared she never would grow up? Why would she doubt it?

Just then the engine came to life and the paddles began to make a *plash plash plash* sound which grew to a thunderous roar. Emma Jane dropped the knife with a clatter onto the plate.

'We're off again,' Jamie said, cheering.

The three ran to the deck, and there, looking at the banks, Matt realised they were turning about to go downstream.

'You're going home,' Emma Jane said.

'Aw, already?' grumbled Jamie.

Matt shared his disappointment. They had only just started their adventure. Why did they have to go back home? Emma Jane didn't look too happy either.

'Let's have breakfast,' she said.

Matt put the problem from his mind. Food came first. He was fading away. 'May I have my boiled eggs now?' he asked.

'We're having scones,' Emma Jane said firmly, going back to the galley. They went after her.

'She's turning into a bossy boots,' Jamie whispered to Matt.

6
Lockmaster of time

MATT AND JAMIE VISITED the skipper in the
wheelhouse. To make up for upsetting him,
Matt brought a plate of scones and some tea
that Emma Jane had prepared. The skipper let
them into the wheelhouse and smiled at Matt
in a fond, sad way.

'Thankyou, Matt.'

'Can I take the wheel while you have your
tea?' Jamie said.

'Would you like to?'

'I wouldn't mind. I'd love it,' he said, taking
his place at the helm. It was as big as a
cartwheel.

'Do you run this whole boat by yourself?'
inquired Matt. 'Where is your crew?'

'A good crew makes itself invisible,' the skipper said evasively, putting his mug and the
plate on a small shelf beside the wheel. He ate

a scone gratefully.

'Yes, but do they use invisible wood, too?' Matt asked. 'Because the pile of wood on the deck hasn't been touched. My dad told me that a paddleboat like this would use a quarter of a ton of redgum an hour and that a ton would only take a boat sixteen kilometres. Boats like this have to stop and load wood every four hours. He also said the wood couldn't be too green or it clogged up the internals. I wonder how your fireman can tell if the redgum logs are too green, if the logs are invisible?'

'I see you did listen to some of the things your father told you,' the skipper said, a look of surprise enlivening his eyes.

'I loved his stories. I'll always remember them. Even when I'm grown-up. I'll probably tell my own children about them one day.'

The skipper picked up his mug of tea. A drop spilt over the lip of the mug and hit the wooden floor like a brown tear, making a spangle.

'And how do you think you'll feel when your own children grow up?' the skipper said. 'Don't you think it will make you sad?'

'Yes, but it will be fun, too,' Matt said, 'to see them getting as big as me. They'd be more like friends then.'

His new friend Jamie was swinging on the wheel as if he were trying to hold it steady in a big sea. 'Steady,' the skipper said. 'You only need to make small adjustments. The thing you learn about paddleboats is that they never go in a straight line. You have to keep making corrections.'

'Can we go round in a circle?' Jamie said.

'Not now. Look ahead.'

A barrier ran across the width of the river. They were approaching a weir and a lock. Strange. Matt didn't remember going through locks in the night. Had they gone through while he slept?

'I'd better take over the helm,' the skipper said.

The gates of the lock opened and the *Return*'s paddles slowed. They drifted into a large chamber. A uniformed official appeared at the edge of the lock and waved them to the side. Then unseen hands threw a line ashore and the man secured it to a bollard.

The skipper stopped the engines and opened a window in the wheelhouse.

'Good morning, Lockmaster,' he said, leaning out of the window.

'Good, you think? We'll see,' the lockmaster said in a creaking voice like a tree toppling over. He was a giant of a man and as straight as a tree trunk. He was dressed in khaki and he wore wrap-around mirror sunglasses that hid his eyes. He also wore a red cap with a flap at the back like that of a French Foreign legionnaire. 'You may change your mind. This is the first lock of time. There are one or two hidden snags lying ahead of you, I fear. Beyond this lock is the river of snags. The slower you go and the longer you take, the more snags will rise to meet you. Eventually as many as three million snags will choke the river.'

'I love snags,' Jamie said. 'Especially with mashed potato and tomato sauce. But I couldn't eat three million of them. I think.'

'Not those kind of snags. He isn't talking about sausages,' the skipper said softly. 'The snags he's talking about are dangerous obstacles. Redgum logs and branches lying hidden under water. Redgum is resistant to rotting in water and it won't float, so redgum trunks and branches lie hidden under the water like battering rams, waiting to hole the unwary boat. A redgum snag can punch a hole right through a paddleboat's four inch planks and sometimes the only clue to their presence is a few streaks and swirls on the surface of the water that look for all the world like a platypus or a cod swimming underneath. Sinkings are common.'

Matt frowned. Strange, he thought. The explanation was familiar. He seemed to recall his father using almost exactly the same words.

'Are we going to raise three million of them?' Matt said.

The lockmaster must have heard him. 'You must pass between them. You have only three hours before all the snags rise and then you will be caught forever.'

'But how will we see them if they're hidden?'

'With sharp young eyes,' the lockmaster said.

The gates gradually closed behind them and now the level of the water in the lock dropped. The *Return* was sinking lower and lower until the wheelhouse was below the level of the lockmaster and they had to look up to see him. The lockmaster went to a set of controls like a telephone box on a pole and he pressed some buttons.

The gates at the front of the lock slowly opened, the paddleboat's engine rumbled into life and the skipper pushed the telegraph to 'slow speed ahead'. The paddles churned up the water inside the lock chamber. The noise thundered against the walls. They crept out of the chamber and into the river of snags.

7

River of snags

'I'M GOING TO NEED your help, men,' the skipper said.

'We're not men. Yet,' Jamie said.

The skipper smiled. 'Well, you're going to have to act like men. I want you to sit at the bow and keep your eyes skinned for snags.'

'Skinned for snag skins!'

'This is serious, Jamie,' the skipper said. 'Keep your eyes open. Watch for any swirls under the water, even if you think it's just a fish. Signal to me. Do you hear?'

'I'm good at games,' the boy said. I know a computer game just like this one. You have to steer through a whole lot of obstacles. Can I have a go at the wheel?'

'Do as I say,' the skipper said. 'I'm counting on you both, men.'

The boys left the wheelhouse. 'Why does he

keep calling us men?' Jamie asked.

'I think it's because he wishes we were,' Matt said.

They took up positions at the bow, sitting behind the rail with their legs over the edge, and stared into the grey-brown water that slid around the paddleboat. A breeze had come up and it ruffled Matt's dark hair, cooling him.

It should have been perfect, a ride on a real, old paddlewheeler on the river. It should have been perfect, but they had to look out for these rotten snags, Matt thought.

He soon tired of it. The breeze ruffled up little waves that shone in the light and made his eyes feel blurry. They had the empty brown river to themselves — no houseboats, no riverside shacks, nothing. Matt felt different. He was feeling different a lot lately, he seemed to remember. He still loved the river, its mysterious turns and its shimmering reaches and the throngs of willows and gums that lined its banks, but something had changed.

'Maybe I'm too young to be given an important job like this,' he thought. 'What if I miss a snag and it sinks the boat? It'll all be my fault.'

The girl slid into a spot beside him.

'Hi,' he said, glad to see her. 'We're looking for snags. Maybe you can help.' She was a responsible girl. Let her take over.

A bream jumped out of the water. Jamie gave a yell to the skipper and pointed. Immediately the skipper slowed the engine and swung the wheel hard. The *Return* heeled over.

'Why did you do that?' Matt said to Jamie.

Jamie scowled. 'The skipper said we should tell him if we see anything, even if it looks like a fish. That looked like a fish. Almost exactly.'

'It was a fish.'

'That's what I thought.'

'We're supposed to dodge *snags*, not fish.'

'Well, you look out for the next one. At least I've seen something.'

'I don't want to. I'm tired of this. Emma Jane, you take over.'

She shook her head, her eyes held his gravely. 'Matt, listen to me,' she said in an earnest tone. 'You've got to grow up. Now. Or you never will. You've got to help the skipper. He's counting on you to save this boat.'

'But I'm just a kid.'

'And that's all you'll stay if you fail.'

Matt was puzzled. This wasn't much fun. The pressure was scaring him. 'Won't you do it instead?' he said.

'No, it's your responsibility. You must do it.' She looked ahead and fright jumped into her face. 'Look out — right now, Matt!'

The urgent note in her voice made him

swing around to see a redgum snag like a sharpened battering ram raising its lethal length to the surface of the water.

'Snag!' Matt yelled, pointing to starboard.

The skipper took swift action, but not swift enough. There was a muffled squeak and a bump, but only a soft one. They went on safely. Matt gulped.

'I've seen one; it's your turn,' he said to Jamie.

'I don't want a turn.'

Matt screwed his eyes shut. 'Well, you've got one. I've closed my eyes, so you'd better take your turn.'

'I'll close mine, too. Look, I already have.'

'Are you two mad?' Emma Jane said angrily. 'Do you think the snags won't come because you've closed your eyes? You're acting like small children. You've got to face the dangers or the *Return* will end up at the bottom of the Murray and you'll go down with her.'

'Matt has to open his eyes first,' Jamie said.

'No, you first,' Matt said. But he remembered the redgum snag they had just bumped against — it could have sunk them. Was another one lying ahead of them right now?

He opened one eye. Ahead were two redgum snags, just beneath the surface, about ten metres apart.

Shall I pretend I haven't seen them? It would serve Jamie right if I closed my eye again, he thought. It would serve Emma Jane right and the skipper, too.

Why should I carry all the responsibility?

He thought of Emma Jane's words:

'Do you think the snags won't come because you've closed your eyes? You're acting like small children. You've got to face the dangers or the Return will end up at the bottom of the Murray and you'll go down with her.'

'Snags!' Matt yelled and he pointed with both hands to the two lurking dangers.

The *Return* heeled over and her nose swung around between the redgum snags. They passed narrowly between them, leaving little more than a few metres clearance on each side.

Matt gave a shivery sigh.

'Well done, Matt,' Emma Jane said. 'I knew you could do it. You saved us.'

'That's positively my last one. Your turn, Jamie.'

'I saw it, too.'

'You didn't say anything.'

'I was waiting.'

'Well, you shouldn't play chicken with snags.'

'Chicken with snags! Don't talk about food. You're making me hungry.'

Matt watched the river ripple towards them. He lifted his eyes and peered a little further ahead. Was it an illusion caused by reflections or were there now snags rising all over the river? They were standing up, like bristles in a hairbrush — except these bristles wouldn't bend. They would tear a hole through four inch planks and let the brown water gush in.

'Snag!' Jamie yelled. 'Snag, snag, snag, snag. . .!'

'Where?' Matt said.

'Everywhere. Almost. Look around!'

'That doesn't help much, Jamie. It's not the ones that are everywhere that we have to worry about. It's the snags that are in front of us that we have to look out for.'

'Oh,' he said, relaxing.

They leaned forward on the rails, staring into the rippling water, and Matt remembered another time when he had stared at the water sliding around a hull, a different hull, a square one on a houseboat. It was a long time ago, a different age. He had seemed much surer of himself then. Yet he'd been unhappy.

What had made him unhappy? Maybe it was caused by the same situation that was bothering him now, a sense of taking on more worry than he was ready to accept. It was scary accepting responsibility. Did you ever feel ready to take it?

A long swirl stretched the skin of the water as if somebody had pulled a thread in a piece of material. A fish? he wondered. Or another snag? He saw another swirl next to that and another beside that. A row of shapes under the surface. Must be a school of fish swimming towards them.

He remembered what the skipper had said:

'. . .sometimes the only clue is a few streaks and swirls on the surface of the water that look for all the world like a platypus or a cod swimming underneath. Sinkings are common. . .'

'Snags!' he yelled, pointing in a line to indicate a row of obstacles.

The *Return* took evasive action, clawing her way around. But it was too late — they couldn't avoid them. They were going to sink. Matt tightened his grip on the rails, cowering to await the bang as they struck.

The school of fish broke around their bow and darted away. One jumped into the air and flashed its silver side like a mirror in the morning sun.

'Fish snags!' Jamie said contemptuously.

Matt let out another shaky sigh of relief. This latest scare was too much for him. He wanted to give up right then and there. He tried to get up, but Emma Jane put a firm hand on his shoulder. 'Don't give up, Matt. I believe in you and your future. I want you to reach it and enjoy it, the way I never will.'

Her voice made him shiver. She said creepy things, this strange girl in the creepy, granny clothes, but this was no time to ask questions.

He turned back to the water and saw snags marching in against the *Return* — an army of them now. Matt spotted a gap between them.

'Snags!' He pointed to the left and to the right of them, indicating a channel. The skipper followed his instructions promptly.

He's trusting me, Matt thought. I almost wish he wouldn't. 'It's scary,' he said aloud. 'I could be wrong.'

'Don't worry about being wrong,' Emma Jane advised him. 'Just concentrate on being right.'

Matt did. But it was awfully hard. His mind kept straying to tiddlywinks of all things. Tiddlywinks was fun, not like this. Games were so much more fun than life. Maybe that was it. It gave him an idea. Perhaps it would be easier if they made a game of it.

'Let's pretend we're playing a computer game,' Matt said to Jamie. 'It's called Attack of the Snagmen. We've got to dodge their explosive warheads.'

Jamie's eyes brightened. 'That sounds okay. Brilliant. Me first. Snagman over there!' Jamie yelled, spotting a redgum stake that speared the surface. The captain swung the wheel, adjusting their course to avoid it. 'Snagman!' Jamie called again. He was getting into the spirit of the game.

'Two snagmen!' Matt shouted.

'Three, actually,' Jamie said, pointing them out.

'Now you're thinking, Matt,' Emma Jane approved.

The river of snags was a fearsome gauntlet, but it was no match for two boys in a computer game. The *Return* wove her way between the snags like a snake between clumps of grass.

The straight line of another weir and lock rose ahead of them. 'We've won!' Matt said.

Jamie cheered. 'Three million points to us! Zero to the snagmen!'

'Some boys will stay boys!' Emma Jane said, shaking her head.

Matt stood up. The belt of his jeans was digging into his stomach for some reason. He undid the belt and let it out a notch. That felt better. It was a good feeling winning, but he felt a bit shaky on his feet.

8

Willow tears

'GOOD DAY, LOCKMASTER,' the skipper said through the wheelhouse window. The lockmaster had tied them up to a bollard inside the lock chamber.

The lockmaster was a willowy, stooped, sorrowful-looking man. He had a handkerchief in his hand and a catch in his voice.

'Not a good day, not good at all. Very sad in fact, as you'll discover.' He blew his nose with a rasp. 'This is the second lock of time,' he said. He gave a sniff. 'Beyond this lock is the river of willows. A crying shame, I'm afraid. Here you will find the river narrows and the willows will reach out their arms to clasp you. As you go further they will grow thicker and their arms more clingy until they bring your boat to a stop in their embrace. You will be unable to go further.'

'Then how do we get through?' the skipper said.

'You must make them break their hold and to do that they must. . .' The man gave a sniff and a choked sob.

'Must what?'

'Break down and cry.'

'Willows cry?'

'I've never heard of a tree crying,' Jamie said.

'Hardly ever.'

'Don't you know about willows?' Matt said. 'Some are called weeping willows.'

'I know that.'

'How do we make trees weep?' the skipper said.

'A sad, sad story, I'm afraid,' the lockmaster replied. 'Very, very sad.' He said no more, but let them through and walked away, blowing his nose.

The paddlewheeler went through the lock and into the second stretch of the river.

Willows leaned over the banks like a crowd pressing close with eagerness to see a sight. The skipper, Matt and Jamie watched from the wheelhouse as the banks slowly converged.

'Look at them,' the skipper said. 'They're stretching out to reach us.'

It was true. Long, drooping branches of the willows were lifting themselves, questing the air like the feelers of insects and those that trailed in the water were snaking towards their hull.

The skipper slammed the telegraph to 'full ahead'. 'Let's see if a willow branch can stop us at full speed,' he said. 'If this boat can tow a line of barges, no stringy willow tree is going to hold us.'

The paddles thundered. But it wasn't one branch and it wasn't one tree that reached out to them. As the morose lockmaster had warned them, the river quickly narrowed and the willows multiplied, almost climbing over each other's shoulders in their eagerness to reach the steaming *Return*.

Long branches like vines wrapped themselves around the crane on the front deck. They drew taut and snapped with a twang and a swishing sound like breaking wires as the *Return* stubbornly pushed on, her paddles ploughing up the surface of the river.

More branches snaked around them, around the wheelhouse and the crane and the deckhouse, even threading through the rails.

'We'll rip apart if we keep going,' the skipper said. 'We'll have to stop and cut our way free. There are some axes near the engine pit.' He shut down the engine and they drifted to a halt.

Branches squeaked and squealed on the roof.

They ran from the wheelhouse to collect the

axes. The skipper handed one to each of them and they set to work, but no sooner had they hacked through one willow branch than another took its place.

The willows were all around them now. Branches on either side of the bank had linked boughs above them, making a cavern that plunged them into deep shadow.

They hacked at the willow branches. The axes were heavy and Matt and Jamie soon tired. They rested while the skipper kept working, swinging the axe desperately. At last he, too, tired. He squatted to rest on the deck, breathing heavily from his exertions.

'We're beaten this time.' he said. 'The lockmaster was right. It's a very, very sad story, for here we stay. Nothing can save us.'

That's when Emma Jane came out onto the deck. 'Only a very sad story will save us,' she said.

'Who are you?' the skipper asked.

Matt was surprised. Hadn't he seen the girl before?

'Don't you know? This is Emma Jane,' Matt said.

Emma Jane went to the bow where the willows were at their thickest. 'We must make the willows weep and only a very sad story will do that. I will tell it for I have that story.'

Emma Jane stood at the bow, surrounded by a throng of willows. Matt and Jamie and the skipper watched and listened, mystified. The willows stooped even closer to listen and rustled their leaves expectantly, like a crowd settling before a performance.

'*Sh-sh* and listen,' she said to the willows. 'It's the story of a young girl, a disaster and a ghost. The girl's name was Emma Jane, just like mine. . .'

She took a deep breath. Then, while the imprisoning willows listened, she began to speak — or was it chant, Matt wondered — in a strange way that wasn't quite poetry, wasn't quite prose, wasn't quite storytelling and wasn't quite song.

The chant of *Emma Jane*

Emma Jane was a riverboat
as every riverchild knew.
She spoke her name in smoke and sparks
and in the steam she blew.
It wasn't just her whistle
that gave away her name,
but the pant of her exhausts
that told them when she came.
    Stay this young, Emma Jane;
    stay this young, Emma Jane.

These were the words they fitted
to the sound of her great stack,
though still unseen behind a bend
away in the outback:
   Stay this young, Emma Jane;
   stay this young, Emma Jane.

Her skipper was a riverman,
the master of the boat,
proudest man and father
that ever went afloat.
He loved his paddlewheeler,
every creak of her jarrah beams,
but the thing he loved the most
was the daughter of his dreams.

He took her on his journeys,
he held her in his eye.
He'd watch her play upon the deck
and like his boat he'd sigh:
   Stay this young, Emma Jane;
   stay this young, Emma Jane.

The skipper was a godly man,
he taught his daughter well.
He took her to a riverchurch,
that called out with its bell.
He taught her how to pray to God,
how to sing his praise.

This was how he dreamed
that they would spend their days.
'But the golden time must end, I fear,'
said a churchman and a friend.
'The city has a ladies' school
that Emma should attend.
The shoot must leave the stem
to start a whole new life.
(Did you not leave your parents
to cleave unto a wife?)

'She must grow in graces,
as every young girl should,
to prepare herself for living,
to reach her womanhood.
So leave her here with us —
my wife will take her there;
you need not leave your boat or stay,
but place her in our care.'

But the skipper's heart was hardened
as he went back to the water.
'I cannot let her go from me,
my precious little daughter.'
       Stay this young, Emma Jane;
       stay this young, Emma Jane.

He started up the engine,
he threw on wood to burn.

He gave the boat full throttle
and made the paddles turn.
He watched her from the wheelhouse,
standing by the mast.
I'll keep things as they are, he thought,
I'll hang onto the past.
If only we keep steaming,
this golden time will last.
    Stay this young, Emma Jane;
    stay this young, Emma Jane.

All day he steamed the river,
through a shimmering heat haze,
then on into the darkness
where his lamps threw yellow rays.
Between the ghost gum groves,
and forests of moonlight,
the *Emma Jane* went throbbing,
throbbing through the night.

A hot wind blew across her bow
and caused a spark to glow,
in among the boiler wood
stacked to make her go.
The *Emma Jane* was burning,
burning in the night.
Flames beat round the wheelhouse,
her timbers were alight.

The captain heaved the wheel around
to take her to the shore.
The crew fought flames with water,
which made her burn the more.
The deck was now a funeral pyre,
the blaze was high and wild,
and through the sundering fire and smoke
he saw his darling child.

He could not reach his daughter
beyond the wall of flame,
though he dared to face its heat
and called out loud her name.
The first mate grabbed him by the arm
and took him, jumping clear:
'Too late, you've lost your heart's desire —
all that you hold dear.'

Round she went, a vessel spent,
her cargo glowing embers.
How long she kept on circling,
no man alive remembers.
The *Emma Jane* was burning,
burning in the night.
And her paddles went on churning,
churning with all their might.

Emma Jane was a paddleboat
as every riverchild knew.

She spoke her name in smoke and sparks
and in the steam she blew.
It wasn't just her whistle
that gave away her name,
but the pant of her exhausts
that told them when she came.
    Stay this young, Emma Jane;
    stay this young, Emma Jane.

These were the words they fitted
to the sound of her great stack,
though still unseen behind a bend
away in the outback:
    Stay this young, Emma Jane;
    stay this young, Emma Jane.

Emma Jane would not grow old,
the captain's vow came true,
a vow he had made selfishly,
a vow he should now rue.
But to this day, he journeys
aboard a ghostly *Emma Jane*,
paddling the river
to find his child again. . .

Dreaming in his wheelhouse
that she plays beneath his mast —
'If only we keep steaming,
this golden time will last.'

But in running from the future. . .
he lost her to the past.

Matt swallowed hard. The skipper sniffed.
Jamie gave a big gulp.

Something was happening, Matt noticed.
Drizzle was falling from the canopy of willow
branches and the leaves were shivering as if in
a breeze. Big raindrops were falling on the
deck making spangles there like tears. The
willows shook their shoulders, the branches
squeaked and stirred.

The willow trees were crying, Matt thought,
impossible as it seemed. Who was this girl, he
wondered.

When she turned, her eyes were filled with
tears. The skipper dried his own eyes on his
sleeve.

'That's not a story I'll forget, Emma Jane.'

'It's quite sad,' Jamie said. 'It's the saddest
story I ever heard.'

Emma Jane fled to the deckhouse.

'We must hurry while there's time to escape,'
the skipper said. They ran with him to the
wheelhouse and he rammed the telegraph to
'full steam ahead'. The sidewheels roared. The
Return broke through the damp clutches of the
willows.

Their hold broken, the long, rope-like

branches swished over the deckhouse and fell trailing into the river.

They left the deep shade and came out blinking into bright sunshine again.

'Emma Jane!' Matt ran along the upper deckhouse, banging on the doors. She emerged, looking composed and gave him a wan smile. She had dried her eyes.

'Are you all right, Emma Jane?'

'It's nice of you to worry about me, Matt. It shows you're growing up. Yes, I'm all right.'

'You seemed so upset as if you knew the girl Emma Jane in the story, almost as if. . .'

'I was Emma Jane? Well I am. . .'

'Yes, but that Emma Jane. . .'

'. . .is dead. And I'm here, so forget about it. . .' She came out of the berth and leaned against the rail, her brown hair billowing out from underneath her Alice band.

'Yes, but how did you know about her?' he said.

'I suppose there's a bit of Emma Jane in all of us who are growing up and whose parents would like us to stay the way we are. Your own parents felt the same, you said.'

Matt shrugged. 'I don't worry about that now. I don't care if I stay the way I am. I'm happy being a kid.'

'You are at the moment,' Emma Jane said.

'But as time goes on and the *Return* draws nearer to her destination and you to yours, you'll feel differently. I can see you're changing already.'

'Is it true that you can fit words to the sound of a paddle-steamer's exhausts? What does the *Return* say?'

'Listen. You tell me.'

Matt put his head on one side and listened to the pant of the exhaust above the *flog flog flog* of the paddle-floats hitting the water.

'I don't know.'

'Listen carefully. *Matthew Stone, get back home; Matthew Stone, get back home.*'

'How do you know my second name?'

'You must have told me. . .'

'I don't think I did.'

'Then maybe I heard you telling Jamie.'

'You said a funny thing at breakfast. You said you can't see yourself growing up. Did you mean you can't picture yourself growing up or you don't think you will grow up?'

She frowned in surprise. 'You're a sharper boy that you seem.'

'Well, what did you mean?'

'Never mind. I think we should have lunch before any of us gets any older. Can you face scones again?'

'Is that all you've got?'

'It's all I know how to make. There are some strange tin barrels in the cupboard, but I don't know how to open them.'

'Cans? Everyone knows how to open cans.'

'Maybe I'm just trying to trick you into giving me some help,' she said smiling.

Matt frowned. Her explanation didn't quite satisfy him. Sometimes it seemed that Emma Jane came from another age. She didn't know about computer games and now she was puzzled by cans.

Was she pretending? Or had she truly stepped out of a museum? The girl's old fashioned long dress and boots and the Alice band in her hair still bothered him. She didn't wear them with the novel air of somebody dressed in costume. She seemed comfortable in them. Emma Jane was like his father, somebody who had been born in the wrong century.

They went to the galley and she opened a small cupboard.

'These,' she said. 'They have lovely pictures of food on them, but no lids.'

She took out two cans, one of cold meat and another of baked beans. 'I've tried twisting them every way.'

She's joking, Matt thought. He opened a drawer and scratched around. His eye fell on a can opener, a modern affair with a butterfly handle. He held it out to Emma Jane.

'Try this.'

She blinked at it. 'Why are you giving me that?'

She was going to play the joke to the end. Perhaps she was one of those girls who liked to pretend she was helpless.

'It's a can opener.'

'But I already have one,' she smiled sweetly.

'What do you mean?'

'You.'

'Oh.' She was teasing him, that was it. Matt shrugged and opened the cans for her while she found some plates. He hoped she was teasing him. The alternative was spooky.

'The first time I saw you, when I went by on the houseboat, I thought you were a ghost in those old clothes. You disappeared so quickly.' He tipped the cold meat, leg ham, onto a plate.

'And what do you think now?'

He looked up to find her eyes regarding him gravely.

'I think you're a bit spooky in those clothes. What do you wear when you're out of costume? Do you wear jeans?'

'Jeans?' She looked blank.

'There you go again. Stop teasing me,' he said.

9

Mist of uncertainty

THE RIVER BANKS MELTED.

It seeped out of the trees and drifted over the waters to reach them, a dense river mist that struck cold deep inside their bones, even in the shelter of the wheelhouse.

Matt shivered. The windows blurred and threw a cold grey light onto the figure of the skipper at the wheel. The mist thickened rapidly.

'The next lock's coming up,' he said, peering ahead. 'Not a moment too soon. Any later and we'd have run right into it.' The skipper slowed the engine.

Matt rubbed the wheelhouse window with the palm of his hand. It made no difference. He squinted through. Ahead, dimly seen, the line of a weir cut the river in half.

'I don't see how we can go on in a mist like

this,' Jamie said. 'At least I don't think I see.'

'You don't see. Nobody sees in a mist like this,' the skipper said dryly.

'I see,' Jamie said.

'I don't,' Matt said. 'Not a thing.'

But the skipper seemed to see. He turned the wheel. The lock came into view, gates open, the chamber waiting to receive them.

The *Return* crept into the third lock of time. They didn't see the third lockmaster in the mist. In fact, Matt wondered if he really existed. All they saw was a vague, moving shape in a grey raincoat. The skipper opened the wheelhouse window as the man secured them to a bollard. Mist drifted into the wheelhouse.

'What now?' the skipper said to the figure in the mist.

There was a long pause. 'Who can say?' a grey, colourless voice replied out of the mist.

'What lies ahead of us, Lockmaster?'

'Who knows?'

'Don't you know?'

'Can't say.'

'What are the challenges?'

The voice had a shrug in it. 'It's hard to be certain.'

'Can you be more clear?'

'Yes and no. You are going into the river of uncertainty and it's not very clear what will happen to you.' The man was as vague as the mist surrounding him.

'I know what he means. I think,' Jamie said. At least Jamie understood him. Maybe that was because Jamie was always particularly vague himself. Jamie had finally met someone as unsure as himself.

'What should we look out for?' the skipper said.

'Them.'

'Them. Please be more specific.'

'It's hard to put a name to them. What shall I call them? Ghost gum people? Mist mirages?'

'What are ghost gum people and mist mirages?' Matt said.

'What indeed?' the figure in the grey raincoat said. Was he still there or was he just a denser accumulation of mist? The lockmaster was maddeningly vague. Matt rubbed his eyes.

The gates of the chamber closed and the level of water in the chamber dropped, taking them down with it. They could no longer see to the other end of the lock. The mist had gathered like grey cotton wool over the lock. They waited. They stopped falling. They were below the edge of the lock now. 'May we pass through your lock now?' the skipper called up.

'Suit yourself. Good luck, I suppose. You'll

probably need it.' The figure in grey withdrew, swallowed up by the mist.

'Cheerio, see you later,' Jamie called after him. 'Maybe.'

'I couldn't see him now, let alone later,' Matt complained.

The skipper took the paddleboat cautiously out of the lock and into the river of uncertainty.

Ghost gum people? Mist mirages? What were these things, Matt wondered. He was soon to find out.

'I'll need you two to leave the wheelhouse and stand at the prow again,' the skipper told them. Matt gave Jamie an uneasy glance. Not that again. 'You'll have to stay out there and keep a sharp eye ahead. See that we don't drift too close to the bank and run aground. Also keep an eye open for snags.'

'We're not going out on the deck with those things out there,' Matt said defiantly.

'I'm afraid you'll have to, men,' the skipper said. 'If we run aground we really will be at the mercy of the river. You should be safe enough, provided you keep your eyes sharp. Arm yourselves with axes if you like.'

Matt felt rebellion rise up inside him, but he saw no sign of it in Jamie's eyes. Jamie seemed quite relaxed. Matt was going to have to mutiny on his own.

'Why don't *you* go and stand out there and we'll take the wheel?' Matt said in a resentful tone.

'Negotiating a river in the mist is tricky enough without leaving it to a pair of boys.'

'I thought we were men,' Matt said acidly.

'Then act like men. I'm counting on you. I'll leave the wheelhouse windows open. Just yell out "port" or "starboard" wherever you see an obstruction and I'll swing the other way.'

'What if there are no ports?' Jamie said, looking vague.

'He means left or right,' Matt said.

'Oh. I knew that. Port is sailor's talk, right?'

'No, it's left,' the skipper said, making a joke to lighten the tension of the situation.

'Right,' Jamie said uncertainly. 'I get it. I hope.'

'Just shout "left" or "right",' the skipper decided wisely.

The skipper returned his attention to the wheel as if the matter were settled. Matt looked at Jamie. Jamie shrugged. 'Let's do it. I reckon,' Jamie said. Jamie left the wheelhouse and Matt followed grudgingly.

The mist took Matt in a clammy embrace as he went out onto the upper deck. He threw a glance over the rail. He could barely see the water below. He followed Jamie along the deck

and down the companionway to the lower
deck. Mist was rolling over the kauri planking.
They picked their way to the bow, stopping on
the way to collect two axes. The weight of the
axe was comforting in Matt's hands.

Ghost gum people, mist mirages. Matt
shivered again. He was glad of the survival
value of the axe. He followed Jamie to the rail
and stood right beside him.

'I don't think we should stand together,'
Jamie said. 'Go to the other side. You watch
one side and I'll watch the other.'

'But we should stay in sight of each other.'

'That all depends on the mist,' Jamie said.

Matt took up a position at the rails on the
starboard side, near the broad flare of the bow.
He could make out the dim shape of Jamie in
the mist. Jamie put the axe over his shoulder
like a sentry shouldering a rifle.

He hoped his new friend would keep guard
properly and not shut his eyes the way he had
done during their passage through the river of
redgum snags. Forget about Jamie. Keep a
lookout yourself.

Matt stared into the mist. He knew how
suddenly a bend could come up on the river.
One minute the riverboat could have a broad
brown river ahead of it, the next it could be
ploughing into a forest of gums, smashing the

deckhouse and splintering its paddleboxes.

The paddles made a different sound in the mist. The skipper held their speed at 'slow'. The beat of the floats had a hollow, enclosed, twisted sound that seemed to beat back at their ears as if bouncing off the mist. The steam-engine's stack above their heads panted in a wheezing way as if struggling to breathe in the swirling greyness. Matt turned his head to check on Jamie.

They must be nearing the bank. Matt saw the pale gleam of a ghost gum near Jamie's side. The boughs of the tree split the greyness of the mist like a flash of branch-lightning in a storm-filled sky. Then he saw that the edges of the branch ended not in twigs, but in hands with extended fingers. The ghost gum reached out for Jamie with long, skeletal wooden fingers that were about to close around him and snatch him off the deck.

Matt ran to Jamie's side, sliding his hands down the handle of the axe, ready to swing at the attacker. Jamie still hadn't seen the danger.

'Look out,' Matt yelled.

'Right or left?'

'Behind you!' The ghost gum's fingers were tightening.

Matt swung the axehead with all his might and hit the white hand at the wrist. There was a rattling crack like bones given a shaking. The fingers shattered and dropped away into the river.

'What did you do that for?' Jamie said. 'It was only a branch.'

'You wouldn't think so if you'd seen it. It was more than a branch. It was a hand reaching out to grab you.'

'A hand in a tree? You're seeing things. You worry about your own side,' Jamie said. 'I'll worry about mine.'

'I'm telling you I saw something.'

'You want to be on this side? Then you take this side. I'll take yours.'

'If you like.'

They swapped. Perhaps it was better to be on this side. The bank must be near if ghost gums were coming into view. Perhaps the paddleboat should alter course and move back into the river. He'd better warn the skipper.

'Left!' Matt shouted to the skipper who immediately took evasive action and swung away.

He swung them straight into the waiting arms of another ghost gum. This time it wasn't a hand reaching out for Jamie — it was two arms with outstretched fingers. Again, amazingly, Jamie hadn't seen it. Matt gave a warning yell and charged Jamie. Jamie swiftly sidestepped and Matt ran into the waiting arms of the ghost gum. He felt hard fingers close with a dry crackle of bones around his waist and he gasped as he was swept clear of the deck.

'Are you mad, grabbing trees? You'll get stuck up there,' Jamie said, dropping his axe and making a lunge for Matt's foot. Matt felt hands grab around his ankle. He felt a hard yank. The ghost gum tightened its grip. Jamie threw all his weight on Matt's ankles. Matt felt his body being stretched. The bones of the ghost gum cracked. Jamie pulled him free. Matt dropped and landed heavily on the deck.

He was free. The ghost gum swept away in the mist.

'Thanks,' Matt said with a shake of relief in his voice.

'You don't have to be funny.'

'I'm not. I really mean thanks. That ghost gum branch was trying to grab at us.'

'No it wasn't. You jumped into it. I saw you. This is not time to climb trees, Matt.'

'Why won't you listen to me?' Matt said despairingly. 'You don't believe me, do you? That ghost gum tree was *alive*.'

'I thought they were called ghost gums because they were dead.'

'They are, but these aren't. They're trying to grab us off the deck. We're going to have to be extra careful. Maybe we should stand together.'

'You're pretty jumpy, aren't you?'

The two boys stood back to back at the prow, watching the mist shred around them. Settle, Matt told himself. Maybe the mist was playing tricks with his eyes. Keep watch. Where was the river bank? There was no sign of it. Should he warn the skipper to move away from this latest obstacle? How narrow was the river here? He hoped the ghost gums weren't marching into the river to meet them.

Matt bent over the rail to search for the river bank. It was bending that saved him. A branch reached out of the mist for him, missed him and grabbed Jamie, hoisting him into the air.

'Hoy!' Jamie yelled. 'Stop that.'

Matt dropped his axe and made a grab for Jamie's sneakers. He missed. Jamie swung out of reach. With the forward motion of the boat, he slipped past Matt.

Matt saw the bisecting masts of the deck crane opened up like insect grabs. One of the arms leaned back towards the deckhouse. He jumped onto it and ran along it. It was slippery from the mist. He skidded, swayed, almost tumbled. Jamie was slipping out of reach. Too far to reach already. He'd have to dive after him. Matt sprang like a trapeze artist, taking

Jamie by the ankles. He clung to the ankles, swinging with Jamie, and for a moment Matt thought they must both be snatched from the deck of the paddleboat. Should he let go? He didn't have to. The ghost gum arms cracked. Jamie broke free. Matt dropped and Jamie fell on top of him.

'Thanks,' Jamie said.

'That's all right. I had to save you.'

'No, I mean thanks a lot,' Jamie said bitterly, 'for hoisting me up on the deck crane. Why did you play a dumb trick like that on me?'

'I didn't.'

'Oh yeah,' Jamie said cynically. 'I suppose another ghost gum tree tried to steal me away.'

'It did.'

'Let's keep watch and stop fooling around, or you can do this on your own. Promise? Say you promise or I'll go.'

Jamie meant it. If he didn't agree that second, Jamie was going to leave him alone out here. Maybe it would be easier alone. He wouldn't have to look after Jamie, a part of his mind whispered.

'I promise,' he said. He didn't want to be out here alone.

He saw a stand of trees coming into view on the port side. They were approaching a bend in the river.

'Left!' he yelled to the skipper. They rounded a bend and went into a broader section of the river. The ghost gums had gone.

There was a slight gap in the mist ahead. It revealed a bubbling disturbance in the river. Matt gaped. A slimy, mud-encased shape that looked to Matt like a deckhouse emerged and, after it, the decking and rotting hull of a riverboat pointed towards them.

'Right!' Matt yelled. The skipper swung away from the shape. As they drew level with it, it sank again, just as quickly, bubbling and hissing and trailing green weeds. Mist closed around the spot where it had been.

'What was that?' Matt said.

'Probably just mud bubbling to the surface. I suppose.'

'Mud? With a deckhouse and a hull? That was a riverboat.'

'Coming up from the mud? There you go imagining things again. I don't know why you're so scared of this mist. It's the easiest part of the river so far.'

It *was* easy for Jamie. There was nothing here to frighten him. It was all comfortingly vague and shrouded in mist, like Jamie's nature. Jamie looked more at home than he had been at any other stage of their journey, Matt thought.

The mist began to clear. 'I'm bored with this. There's no excitement here,' Jamie said. They went back to the wheelhouse to join the skipper.

'Well done, men. The mist is breaking up,' the skipper said.

'It was easy,' Jamie said. 'There was nothing out there.'

The river of uncertainty had passed Jamie by in a blur. Matt wondered if Jamie always found safety and comfort in his vagueness. Maybe seeing things clearly was too scary for him. But it was dangerous to be like that, he felt. Believing things weren't there didn't take them away. It couldn't take away snags that were lying under the water waiting to hole the unwary boat. It couldn't take away the branches of ghost gums reaching to sweep you off the deck. It was scary seeing the truth, but it was the only way you could survive.

He recalled how he had been tempted to close his eyes in the river of snags and felt a flush of shame. He'd been acting like a kid.

You had to face challenges, even the challenge of uncertainty.

10

River of surprises

IT WAS AFTERNOON before they reached another lock of time. The *Return* ran bravely to meet it. What would their next obstacle be, Matt wondered.

'This is the fourth and final lock of time,' the lockmaster told them. 'And this time we throw away the key! Get it?'

He laughed loudly. He was a large, jocular man with a belly that carried on shaking even after the mirth had left his face. 'If this one doesn't lock you in, nothing will. You never know what will hit you next. You just can't pick it. Get it? Pick the lock? Will there be a flood?'

He pointed to a large indicator board that gave details of distance from the river mouth, the pool height above sea level and included a flow indicator recording the river's flow in thousands of megalitres a day. It showed that the river was flowing at 8 000 megalitres.

'In the flood of 1956, the flow was 350 000 megalitres,' the lockmaster told them. 'But the flood you may meet beyond this lock will make that one look like a trickle. And after the flood, what next? Will it be fire, will it be a low river, sandbars and stranding? Disasters? Triumphs? This is the river of surprises.'

He closed the gates of the lock behind them. 'But it's too late to go back. You're well and truly locked in now. Get it?' he said in a jokey voice.

'One final warning. Time is also your enemy. You have only twenty-four hours. You must go back to where you started, before you dropped the coin' — looking accusingly at Matt — 'to that afternoon so long ago when you started your journey, or here you must stay — locked in time!'

The lock gradually drained, the gates opened and they went churning into the river of surprises.

As the wall of the lock receded, another followed them, a wall of angry water. It was as if the entire weir of the lock that dammed the river had suddenly fallen away, releasing a tidal wave of brown water.

'Here it comes; hold on, men!'

The wall of water hit the *Return* and flung her with such force that for a brief moment her sidewheels fanned the air. She landed heavily, water smashing over her stern.

The skipper fought with the wheel. They flew along the river and rounded a bend, their stern sliding out with the current. They were in a spin. The skipper swung the wheel to correct their course.

Another surprise met their eyes around the corner. The river had gone. A water plain opened up around them — a foam-tossed brown expanse that stretched as far as the eye could see, washing away the landscape.

Flood. The first of the surprises.

'We must run with it,' the skipper said. 'But it will make steering difficult. It's also going to make it hard to know if we're in the river or not. Take the wheel, men, while I check my chart to see if I can work out which way the river goes from here.' He pulled down a long narrow chart on a roll to study it. His back was turned.

Matt and Jamie each took hold of the wheel on opposite sides and had a good tussle to see who could pull the hardest, yanking in opposite directions so hard that first Matt's feet left the deck, then Jamie's, as they see-sawed on the wheel.

'Struggling manfully to hold her on course, I see,' the skipper said, turning around again. 'Good men.'

The boys made faces at each other.

The skipper took the wheel. 'It's guesswork from now on. I'll just have to follow my instincts.'

The floodwaters were drowning willows, whole forests of gum trees, obscuring everything. The river was now a brown sea.

'Doesn't your chart tell you where we are?'

'The chart isn't much good if all the landmarks are gone.'

'Can't you use a compass?'

'Fine if the river were a straight line, but it has curves like a rippleskin snake. A compass isn't much help except in a general way. We can easily stray way inland. We might be going cross country right at this moment, going where no paddleboat has ever been before.'

'Does that matter?' Matt said. 'We can save time by going in a straight line instead of following all the curves in the river.'

'As long as the river doesn't drop. If it does, we could find ourselves stuck in the outback paddling the dust.'

'Wouldn't it be fun if we ended up stuck on the freeway somewhere or maybe on somebody's roof!' Jamie said.

'It wouldn't be fun being stuck in time for eternity,' the skipper said. 'And there are no roofs and no freeways that I can see. Haven't you noticed? There's no other soul on this river. No boats. No shacks. We're all alone. . .'

Matt remembered his father telling him the legend of a riverboat being found high and dry miles from any river, left stranded there when the floodwaters fell. Would it happen to them?

The lockmaster had warned of strandings.

But there was little chance of being stranded in this racing torrent of water, Matt thought. There was an ocean around them. It would take weeks for the level to drop.

The *Return* was sweeping past floating branches and treetrunks carried along by the swirling floodwater.

'We must be careful snags don't get into our paddle-boxes,' the captain said. 'They'll smash our paddlewheels and leave us at the mercy of the current.'

The skies grew dark. Lightning split jagged cracks in the sky. Matt brought the skipper lunch — canned meat and beans, and a mug of tea. The skipper wrestled the wheel, eyes anxiously searching the ocean of muddy water that stretched to the horizons.

'Are we in the river?' he mused. 'Who knows? There are no landmarks to guide us.'

Jamie took the wheel while the skipper ate. The big man looked pale and exhausted and Matt recalled that the skipper hadn't slept since they'd left. 'Would you like to have a rest?' he said. 'Jamie and I will take over.'

The skipper shook his head and smiled. 'That's thoughtful of you, Matt, but not in this flood. I'll see us through this patch first. Once I know we're back in the river, perhaps.'

They rode the raging floodwaters all afternoon — then the river surprised them. The *Return* was running like a giant water beetle in a lake of brown water when suddenly treetops rose to the surface. It was as if somebody had pulled out the plug in a bathful of dirty water.

'We'd better make sure we're in the river, fast,' the skipper said. 'The water's dropping like a stone.'

They craned through the wheelhouse window. 'It's like going down in an express elevator,' Matt said, looking around them. Bushes and then rocks emerged from the water.

'The *Return* can smell the bottom,' the skipper said. 'She's sniffing at it like a dog.'

The elevator was about to reach 'ground floor', Matt thought. He felt a bump and he staggered. Shallows dragged against their hull. This couldn't be the river. They had strayed from its course. Where were they?

About a kilometre ahead, to their starboard side, they saw a line of willows. The captain swung the wheel towards it. He swung so sharply that he lifted the paddle-floats on one side clear out of the water.

No sooner had he done it than there were more scraping sounds on the hull. Trees swept past the deckhouse like green icebergs.

'Maybe we'll be stuck at the top of a tree and become a treehouse,' Jamie said. 'That would be wild. I think.'

The *Return* hit bottom a quarter of a kilometre from the river. She stopped and they sat high and dry, surrounded by puddles. The storm receded. A bright, late afternoon sun came shining in great shafts through silver-grey clouds.

'That's it, men,' the skipper said with bitterness. 'Here we stay.'

'For how long?' Jamie asked.

'The last flood like this was in 1956.'

'You mean we're staying here for a while. Forever?'

'Maybe another forty years. Unless somebody can think of something.'

Matt looked through the deckhouse window. There was a pool of deeper water a few metres ahead of them. Could it take them to the river?

'I have an idea,' he said. 'I remember my

father telling me what riverboats used to do when they got stuck.'

Under his direction they jumped off the boat into ankle-deep water and went to check the depth of the pool ahead. The level of the water was no higher than their calves. 'Will it take us?' Matt said.

'It's only about a foot or so,' the skipper said dubiously. 'Maybe a bit more in places. Trouble is, we draw around eighteen inches in the *Return*.'

'Isn't it worth a try?' Matt said. It was his idea and he desperately wanted it to work. He spotted two giant gums standing like sentinels in the pool of water. 'We can use those trees,' he said.

The captain shrugged. 'We don't have any better plans right now.'

The skipper and the two boys tied cables to the paddle drive shafts and jumped off the boat again. They waded back into the pool, taking the cables to the pair of gum trees that rose like piers out of the water. They secured the cables to the trunks of the trees. Then they climbed aboard the paddleboat. Was the level of the water still falling, soaking into the ground? Was it going to be deep enough to carry them?

Back in the wheelhouse Matt looked out of the window. Two cables fanned out from the

Return to join the gum trees. It looked like a catapult and the paddleboat was the stone, he thought. He wished the cables were elastic and could shoot them back into the river.

Cling, cling. The bell rang as the skipper moved the telegraph to 'stand by' and then 'slow speed ahead'. The engine awakened and the paddles turned.

Dish, dish, dish. The floats slapped at the shallow water. It was a different sound; not the usual *boof, boof, boof* they made in deep water. Matt decided to listen for a change in their note. The cables rasped over their bow as the driveshaft wound them in like a windlass. The *Return* creaked as the cables took the strain. The steam engine hauled. They began to stir and move. The tethering trees shivered. The paddleboat was inching towards them, mud sucking at her hull. The boat dug in, hesitated. The cables quivered. Would they break?

'Be careful. If those cables go they'll come cracking over the wheelhouse and could smash through the glass. Broken snag lines have cut men in half.'

The *Return* was tearing herself apart, pulling herself forward with her cables while holding herself back with her weight. Matt stood at the wheelhouse window. He heard the pant of her exhausts. *Matthew Stone, get back home; Matthew*

Stone, get back home.

Would he ever get back home?

The paddleboat gave a loud squelch and jumped forward as if breaking the hold of the mud. Now they were screeching and sliding over the bottom.

They reached the edge of the pool, but the way became no smoother. They were halfway into it now. Matt waited for the blessed lift of buoyancy, or a change in the paddles' note that would signal deeper water, but neither came. The cables were almost taken in fully now. The *Return* was well into the pool.

The skipper leaned over to the telegraph and stopped the paddles.

They were stuck firmly on the bottom.

'Good try, men, but this is as far as we're going.'

Matt slammed the window sill in disappointment. The river was so tantalisingly close. 'We've got to do something,' he said.

'Know what I'm going to do?' the captain said with a heavy sigh. 'I'm going to release those cables and then grab some shut-eye. I'm tired. Wake me if the waters rise. My cabin is the first berth after the wheelhouse, right next door.'

'You're going to sleep now?'

'What else? Believe me, we're in no hurry.

We have all the time in the world. We have eternity.'

He left them and the two boys looked at each other. They were stuck in the mud and in time.

11

River of dew

'WHAT DOES THIS MEAN?' Jamie said.

Emma Jane came into the wheelhouse. 'It means you never grow up,' she said. 'It means you'll never enjoy the futures that lie ahead of you. It means you'll stay forever young, like Emma Jane. . . unless you get back into the river and continue your journey.'

'Yes, but how? We can't push a paddleboat into the river. We can't carry it.'

'Can't you? Come out of the wheelhouse and tell me what you feel.'

The two boys looked puzzled but went with her. Dusk was settling into the bushland, the ratcheting sounds of frogs and insects tuning up for the orchestra of night. The dew was falling like invisible rain.

'What do you notice?' Emma Jane said.

'It's getting dark,' Jamie answered.

'And what else?'

'The dew's falling,' Matt said, putting out his hand.

'Do you remember what your father told you about the dew?'

'Yes, but how do you know?'

'Never mind. Think.'

It was like turning his mind to another age, not back, but ahead to a dimly seen glimpse of the future. . . His mother and Bexie playing cards, his father telling him about redgum snags, about fires, floods and low water, and the riverboats he loved.

Suddenly Matt missed his father and mother and sister, and wanted, more than anything else, to be back with them.

'The dew, Matt,' Emma Jane prompted him. 'What did he tell you about the dew?'

'My dad said that a riverman with faith in his heart could float his riverboat on the dew. . . But that's impossible. It's just a story.'

'Not if you have faith in your heart.'

She was serious. She believed they could ride on the dew.

'It's crazy. I think,' Jamie said.

'Is it?'

Emma Jane regarded the two boys gravely. 'Faith can move mountains, why not a paddle-boat?'

She meant it and something in her manner made Matt believe it too, mad as the idea seemed. He looked around him at the solid mass of the *Return*, felt the firm kauri deck beneath his feet. How many tonnes did the paddleboat weigh? If she couldn't float in this pool of water, how could she float on the dew? He held out his hand again to feel the invisible moisture. Had that much dew fallen? Perhaps the water level had risen beneath them.

He noticed that a night mist was rising. It trickled between the redgum trees, reaching towards their boat. It was like a slow-moving, misty flood.

'I'll wake up the skipper.'

'He won't be awakened,' she said. 'We must do it alone. We three who are gathered here. But we must believe.'

'Believe in what?'

'Not in what. In whom,' she said gently.

'I believe it,' Jamie said. 'I think.'

'Don't think, Jamie. Be *sure* of something for once in your life. All three of us must believe, unwaveringly. Let us bow our heads and believe.'

The three bowed their heads.

Matt imagined the fine mist of the dew gathering in droplets and sliding down their hull. It was running out of the bushland and gathering underneath them, filling the pool, raising them. The *Return* was stirring, coming to life with faint creaks and shiftings.

'Start her,' Emma Jane said.

Matt rammed the telegraph to 'slow speed ahead'.

The *Return*'s paddles rumbled and began to turn. *Dish, dish, dish.* The paddleboat shifted. They were moving between the two gum trees. The branches passed on either side of them.

'Look,' Jamie said. 'We're moving! It's true. I don't believe it. . .'

'Keep believing, Jamie.'

'I do believe, I do. . .'

The *Return* was riding on the dew, carried by the faith of three young hearts, her paddle-floats beating an invisible river of mist and dew. The hulk of the paddleboat moved past more trees half-hidden in the mist. The river was drawing near.

Matt tried to lighten the paddleboat with the power of his will, imagining a million invisible, lifting hands being placed under their hull. He willed the boat to be lighter and more buoyant. He lifted his heels off the deck, standing on tiptoes, as if it would help to lighten the load.

Don't stop now, paddleboat. You're nearly there. He saw Jamie lean forward against the wheelhouse window as if it would help to tip them into the river.

Emma Jane smiled in a satisfied way. The smile seemed to say: 'I told you so.'

Matt took the wheel. He steered towards a gap in the line of willows and the branches parted and squeaked as the paddleboat shouldered its way through. Then they hit water. They were back in the river. *Boof, boof, boof.* The paddlewheels changed their note. It was the full, reassuring sound of the floats finding deep water. Matt and Jamie cheered.

'We did it!'

'Wake the skipper,' Matt said.

Jamie went to rouse him. He banged on his door, but he returned to the wheelhouse a little while later, shaking his head. 'He's asleep. I opened the door and called to him, but he wouldn't wake up. He's snoring a bit. Like a chainsaw.'

'Let him sleep,' Emma Jane said, going to the door of the wheelhouse. She looked back along the river. 'You can say goodbye to him for me.'

'Say goodbye? Where are you going?' Matt said.

'The time has come for me to leave.'

'Take the wheel,' Matt told Jamie hastily. He followed Emma Jane onto the deck.

12

Paddle-Ghost

EMMA JANE LEANED over the rail to peer up the river behind them. 'Look,' she said, pointing back. Matt followed her line of vision. He saw a trail of moonlight on the water. But Emma Jane wasn't talking about the moonlight. He saw the sweep of two long yellow rays in the night.

They weren't alone any more. There was another boat on the river.

Who could it be?

'It's the *Emma Jane*,' she said gravely. 'Goodbye, Matt. My father's come for me. I've been expecting him.'

Matt shivered, but it wasn't because of the night dew. Was she a ghost after all?

'But the *Emma Jane* burnt and sank,' he objected. 'Are there two *Emma Janes*?'

'Yes. Me and a riverboat.'

'What do you mean, Emma Jane? What are you saying?' His skin crawled as if he had walked through a spider's web.

The paddle-steamer was closing on them fast. She was aglow like a fairy castle. Bright sparks showered from her stack. But the glow came from more than her light, more than her two yellow eyes lighting up the river banks ahead of her. Flames from her stern reached into the sky.

'She's on fire!'

'Just as before,' Emma Jane said:

The Emma Jane *is burning,*
burning in the night.
Flames beat round the wheelhouse,
her timbers alight.
The captain heaves the wheel around
to take her to the shore.
The crew fight flames with water,
which makes her burn the more.
The deck is now a funeral pyre,
the blaze is high and wild. . .'

She spoke in an altered voice, the way she had spoken when she had first told the story of Emma Jane:

He cannot reach his daughter,
beyond the wall of flame,

though he dares to face its heat
and calls out loud her name. . .
The Emma Jane *is burning, burning.*
And her paddles go on churning, churning.

'Emma Jane, stop it,' Matt said, shaking her arm. 'You're scaring me.'

But Emma Jane went on. She seemed to be in the grip of a trance:

Emma Jane would not grow old,
the captain's vow came true,
a vow he had made selfishly,
a vow he should now rue.
But to this day, he journeys
aboard a ghostly Emma Jane,
paddling the river to find his child again. . .

'I won't let him have you,' Matt said.

She blinked at him as if coming out of the trance. 'He's calling. Listen.'

The silhouette of a man stood on the burning deck, but he did not face the inferno. He was facing the *Return* and was calling out a name: 'Emma Jane, Emma Jane!'

Matt ran to the wheelhouse to warn Jamie. 'There's a paddle ghost following us. It's the *Emma Jane*. We mustn't let her catch us. They're trying to take Emma Jane.'

'Don't worry, you watch how fast I can run with a ghost behind me,' Jamie said. 'I'm a bit scared of ghosts. Petrified.' He jammed the telegraph to 'full steam ahead', *cling, cling*. He grabbed the wheel and started spinning it around like a little kid in a toy car, as if it would make them go faster.

The *Return's* nose sat up in the river as her sidewheels dug in deep. Matt left him to it. Emma Jane had gone to the rear of the upper deck to watch the approaching fireboat. He ran to join her.

The *Return* pulled away.

'We can't outrun her,' Emma Jane said. 'The *Emma Jane* was the greyhound of the river. She had a massive engine.'

'Yes, but we have Jamie. And he's a massive idiot. Look at the way he's steering!' The *Return* was zig-zagging on the river like a mad water bug. 'She's going to have a hard job catching us!'

'We can't deny him. We can't stop fate from taking its course.'

'Why not? We'll change things. We've floated on the dew. We can do anything tonight.'

'Do you think so, Matt? I don't want to go with them. I want to go ahead with you. I want my future. I want to grow up and have a life and maybe a little Emma Jane of my own one day.'

'Then hang on, Emma Jane, you're in for the race of your life,' Matt said. He darted off towards the engine area. 'I'm taking over the running of this engine, ghost crew or not,' he thought.

Down the metal companionway he went, into the clamour of the engine pit. The hot iron smell of the labouring steam engine hit him like a wall. The pistons were pumping and the big flywheel was spinning in a blur. He looked up.

A gauge said the engine was running at a pressure of seventy pounds per square inch. She was an old boat, but in her day paddleboats such as this could run at higher pressures without blowing, he recalled his father telling him. Maybe she could go up to 100, 120, or even a bit more without blowing. He was going to have to find out. Their pursuers weren't going to get Emma Jane if he could help it.

Matt swung the firebox door open. The heat of the furnace roared out of the red mouth and singed the hair on his arms. It was half-filled with redgum logs, flaming and mottling redly. Who had put them there?

He found a long poker with a right angle bend on one end and shoved it in, stoking the logs and making the flames leap up. More wood. He searched for it. No wood down there. It was stacked on the deck. He swarmed up the companionway and went to the wood pile. He leaned over the rail to check on the *Emma Jane*. She was closing surely.

Matt grabbed a redgum log from a pile. The logs were cut into three foot sections for the burner. He dragged the piece to the edge of the engine pit and then another. Hurry up, he told himself. He heard a steam whistle blasting. The *Emma Jane* was signalling them to stop.

He dropped a log in his fright. Keep going. He dragged more logs to the edge of the engine pit. Then he tossed them over and went down after them.

He swung the firebox open, staying back this time so that the heat would not singe his arms, and he threw a redgum log into the glowing mouth. It threw up sparks and flames. He threw in more logs. Flames leapt hungrily around them. Did he dare add more? He shrugged and threw in the remaining pieces, then shut the firebox door.

Overfiring it was called. He could probably squeeze another three or four horsepower out of the old steam engine, but there was a risk. Would the boiler blow?

He thought of Emma Jane and the blazing

paddleboat and decided to take the chance. Aloft again for more wood, he threw the redgum logs over the railing to make a stack below. The engine hammered and sweated. He added these logs to the furnace and shut the firebox door.

He was sweating. It must have been fifty degrees down there. It was like a sauna. Engineers and firemen must have been the thinnest men on the boat, he thought.

It reminded him of the invisible crew. He glanced around uneasily. Were there unseen eyes watching him, heads shaking at his folly? The engineer would not approve of what he was doing.

'Sorry, men,' he said, but the clamour of the steam engine stole the words from his mouth.

Come on, old engine, faster, faster, Matt thought, willing it to pick up speed. Could it go faster? Perhaps this was its limit. He watched the pumping pistons and the spinning flywheel and the belts like giant bicycle chains driving the paddlewheel shafts.

The needle on the pressure gauge quivered and started to soar. It moved up from eighty to ninety and then a hundred pounds per square inch. His father had told him about disasters on the river where steam engines had exploded. If this boiler went up, it would take the whole superstructure with it, leaving nothing but a flat deck.

How would that save Emma Jane?

Was he being too reckless?

The needle on the gauge hit 130 and a piercing shriek rattled the engine pit, a noise so shrill it drowned out the clamour of the engine. The safety valves howled, unable to keep up.

Would she explode? He looked at the sturdy iron sides of the boiler. Hold, he thought.

Matt climbed out of the engine pit and ran onto the deck. They had pulled away again, but now the *Emma Jane* was putting on more steam and belching flames from her stack. She was still on fire. Flames from her rear deck followed her like an afterburner.

Matt ran up the companionway towards the wheelhouse, pausing at the captain's berth. He banged on the door. There was no reply. He went inside. The skipper lay on his back on a bunk, peacefully asleep.

How could he sleep through this? Couldn't he hear the shriek of the safety valves? Hadn't he heard the whistle of the *Emma Jane*?

'Skipper, you've got to wake up.'

Matt shook the skipper's shoulder. He put his ear to the man's face. Was he breathing? A loud snore made him jump. 'Wake up, please!'

The skipper slept on. Matt left him and

rejoined Jamie who was spinning wildly at the wheel.

'What's that squealing sound?' he said.

'The safety valves. They can't keep up. I've over-fired the boiler to get every ounce of power out of the steam engine and now they're kicking up a racket.'

'Are we going to blow up?'

'Hope not. It would blow us sky high.'

'That's a bit scary,' Jamie said. 'It's terrifying.'

'Don't worry. My father said these boilers can take more pressure than people think. When they're given boiler inspections they're put through a hydrostatic test and tested at up to 240 pounds of pressure per square inch. We're running at 120, so we should be all right with a bit of luck. Just stay ahead of the *Emma Jane*, that's all,' Matt said.

'Will we beat her?'

'We don't have to. Just stay in front of her until she burns and sinks.'

'The way she did in Emma Jane's story? What about the people on board?'

'They're ghosts.'

'Then why do they want Emma Jane?' Jamie must have seen an answer in Matt's face. 'Oh no,' he said in a sinking voice. 'I think I get it.'

'Don't think. Keep going.'

They took the *Return* around a bend, gum trees on the banks glowing grey and ghostly in the beams of her twin headlamps. Jamie took the turn too sharply and their stern slid out. He battled to correct her course and they waddled into the straight.

The overfiring had bought them a few minutes, but the *Emma Jane's* superior speed brought her up. She drew level with them as they neared some cliffs on their port side. She was ablaze now. How much longer could she go on burning before she sank? Would she go into a final spin as she had done in Emma Jane's story? Would everything happen just the way it had happened in Emma Jane's story?

'What can we do?' Jamie said.

'Let me take the wheel. My dad told me about riverboat races. There's a tactic we can use.' Jamie stepped aside. Matt took the helm, swinging the wheel towards the *Emma Jane* and the cliffs.

'What are you doing?'

'Squeezing her up against the cliffs.' The river narrowed ahead at the next turn in the cliffs. 'She's going to run out of river and she'll have to slow.'

'We must be careful she doesn't set us on fire,' Jamie said nervously. Sparks were flying over the water from her raging stern.

'Good thought,' Matt said, taking charge. 'Go out and grab a bucket of water and put out any sparks that hit us.'

'I'm not going out there with a ghost ship travelling beside us.'

'If they catch us, they'll board us to take Emma Jane.'

'I'll do it,' Jamie said.

Matt swung hard towards the *Emma Jane*. The wall of cliffs leaned over the paddleboats. The *Emma Jane* was running out of river. It was going to work. The corner raced up. Only one boat could get through, yet the *Emma Jane* wasn't slowing. Matt gulped. Did she intend to ram the *Return*? It was cooler in the wheel-house than it had been in the engine pit, but Matt was sweating more. Would the captain of the *Emma Jane* dare to ram them with his daughter on board?

The paddleboats seemd to converge. No, it was just the river narrowing. The *Emma Jane* hadn't altered course by a single degree. How did she hope to get through? Maybe she hadn't seen the cliffs or maybe she was out of control. Perhaps the fire in the stern had destroyed her steering.

The *Emma Jane* was doomed.

Matt lost sight of her as the *Return* paddled around the bend and the river opened up in

front of him. He pointed the *Return's* nose back
into the river, pulled the telegraph back to half
speed and they slowed. The safety valves had
stopped their shrieking.

Matt left the wheel for a moment and looked
back towards the bend in the cliffs. He blinked
in amazement. Two long yellow rays emerged
from the sheer wall of rock and the *Emma Jane*
came blazing into view, paddling straight
through the cliff.

'Oh no,' Matt said. The race wasn't over.

The *Emma Jane* could not be stopped.

13

Emma Jane's father

JAMIE MUST HAVE seen it, too. He came back to the wheelhouse looking wild-eyed.

'I'm not staying out there any more,' he gasped.

Matt rammed the telegraph back to 'full ahead'.

'You take over the wheel.' he said to Jamie. 'I'm going to protect Emma Jane.'

He grabbed a boathook and ran to the stern where Emma Jane stood immobile, the glow of the pursuing paddleboat's lights and the glare of the flames illuminating her face.

'We can't get away from them,' she said.

'Surely she's going to burn and sink.'

'Not without me on board.'

'Forget it. They're not going to get you,' Matt said grittily. He had the boathook in his hand and an angry light in his eyes.

'That doesn't sound like the little boy who wanted to play tiddlywinks. I was right. You are changing. You mustn't worry about me. You must think of your own future, Matt, and don't be angry with your parents for wanting things to be the way they were. Just as you're uneasy about the future and need reassurance, so do they. Their only fault is in loving you too much. They don't want your relationship ever to end, that's all. But it needn't and it won't if you're sensible.'

'Are you angry with your father?' Matt asked.

She shook her head. 'How can I be angry with him for loving me too much? But parents, just like children, have to learn to be brave.'

'What will happen if he catches us? Will he come on board?'

'He'll ask me to come back.'

'That's all? Ask? Will you go?'

'He's my father. I must listen to him.'

'Listen all you like. But don't do anything. I'll try to reason with him.'

Matt ran back to the wheelhouse and told Jamie to stop the engine.

'And let the ghost boat catch us? That's not very smart. It's crazy.'

'We can't outrun her.' Matt explained. 'We can't destroy her. And she's not going to burn and sink. She's going to keep coming.'

Matt left the wheelhouse. He saw Emma Jane standing below on the main deck, waiting for her father to come alongside. He joined her, standing beside a now silent paddle-box.

Stay this young, Emma Jane;
stay this young, Emma Jane.

Matt could hear the pant of the pursuing boat's exhausts and the *slap, slap, slap* of her paddles as she drew level. She was a three-decker, with big red paddle-boxes. She cut her engine and drifted towards them.

Matt expected a blast of heat from her fire to hit him like the heat from the firebox in the engine pit, but it was an icy flame that spread towards him. It sent shivers through him.

A tall, bearded man in a blue captain's uniform came out of the fire and the smoke and stood staring at Emma Jane. Meanwhile the fireboat touched the side of the *Return* with a gentle bump and a plank was run out to their deck.

The glow of the flames lit up Matt and Emma Jane like a spotlight. Matt grabbed Emma Jane's arm. It wasn't the arm of a ghost. It was the arm of a warm, living girl.

'Emma Jane.'

'Father.'

'Come back, Emma Jane.'

Matt felt Emma Jane tremble.

'Yes, Father.' She moved towards the gangplank, but Matt's grip tightened around her arm and he pulled her back. He stepped in front of her blocking the way.

'You can't have Emma Jane,' Matt said stoutly, though he was quaking inside.

The captain's eyes glowed like headlamps. They fixed on Matt. The glow in the eyes dimmed and a pair of bright blue eyes came into view. 'And by what power do you stop me from taking my daughter?' he said in a voice like the low roar of flames in a firebox.

Matt scratched around in his brain for an answer, but the answer was there on his lips, before he knew he'd thought of it.

'The greatest power in the world, above it or below it,' he said. 'It is written that a man shall leave his mother and father and cleave to his wife. Just as you did. We were made to live our own lives, not live the wishes of someone else. Now it's Emma Jane's turn to live a life and you've got to let her live it. You've been selfish once; don't go on being that way for all eternity. Please. Let go. I know it's hard.'

It was the same argument the churchman had used in the story of Emma Jane. Would her father listen this time? It was time he learnt, Matt thought, ghost or no ghost.

'And how do you feel about leaving your mother and father one day and beginning a life of your own?' the skipper said in a voice that sighed like logs stirring in a fire.

Matt swallowed. 'I'm a bit scared of it right now. But I know I'll have to be brave and do it. And I know I will always love Mum and Dad — and that love doesn't end; it just changes.'

The ghost of Emma Jane's father blinked at Matt in sad resignation. To Matt's surprise, he bowed his head.

'Father,' Emma Jane said, trying to struggle past Matt.

'Goodbye, Emma Jane,' her father said, looking up again. 'It has taken a young boy with faith in his heart to make me see the truth. I am pierced to my depths with sorrow. Don't stay this young, Emma Jane. Grow up and live your life, just as I lived mine. But try to understand and to forgive me.'

The figure began to fade and, with it, the flaming hulk of the *Emma Jane*.

'I'll always be your daughter,' Emma Jane shouted.

The captain waved and gave a fading smile. Then the *Emma Jane* was gone. Empty water rippled in the moonlight beside them. There was nothing. Not even the smell of smoke.

Emma Jane was weeping. Gently, Matt put his hand on her shoulder. 'We've got to be brave about growing up, Emma Jane,' he said. 'We're going to rejoin the future. And you're coming with us.'

Jamie was gesticulating from the wheelhouse, and Matt went to join him. 'Did I see what I thought I saw?' Jamie asked. He had been peering out of the wheelhouse window.

'We've just seen a ghost. I think,' Matt said, sounding a bit like Jamie.

'You're right. I'm sure we did.'

The *Return* steamed on through the night.

The river turned to gunmetal at first light. Ducks took off from the river ahead of the *Return* and made an arrow in the dawn sky that pointed to home. The sun came up and turned the riverworld golden.

Matt yawned. Jamie was slumped in the corner of the wheelhouse, dozing.

The skipper emerged from his berth scratching his head.

'How did we get here? What are you two kids doing at the helm of my boat? Did the river get up again?'

'Something like that,' Matt said, 'and we've done pretty well so far.'

'Why didn't you call me?'

'You needed some sleep.'

'So do you by the look of you. Off you go.' He gave Jamie a shake. 'Off you go, too, son. Your night watch is ended.'

The skipper stopped Matt as he was leaving the wheelhouse. 'Just a word. I want you to know how proud I am of you, son. You're turning into somebody I can lean on. That's a nice feeling. Sleep well.'

'Thanks.'

Matt left the wheelhouse and found his berth. He wondered whether he should take off his clothes before he went to sleep. The belt of his jeans was digging into him. Maybe the belt needed loosening. He let it out.

That was better. He noticed that the legs of his jeans were riding high on his legs, almost up to his calves. Had they shrunk when he'd waded in the water? The sneakers were squeezing his feet because the laces were too tight. Perhaps they had shrunk, too. Or maybe he was growing. He bent and unrolled the trouser legs and undid the laces. The sneakers fitted perfectly, he noted.

Was he changing?

He remembered the mirror sitting on the shelf — it would tell him the truth. He didn't have to stand on tiptoes to reach the mirror this time. He lifted the silvery surface to his face, looked into it, then sighed in relief. That looked better. But wait, was this the side with the magnification? He flicked the mirror to the other side. His eyes swam in the power of magnification. Then it was true. He was back to normal again.

He put the mirror back on the shelf, kicked off his sneakers, and fell onto his bunk. He had never felt so tired. It was like falling into deep black water.

He sank to the bottom of a dreamless sleep.

14

Friends of the
PS Return

IT WAS AFTERNOON when Matt woke up. He thought of Emma Jane and smiled. They would soon be home.

Up in the wheelhouse the skipper stood turning the big brown wooden wheel, making small corrections to their course.

'You must have needed that, son.'

'I did. Where are the others?'

'Still asleep. I haven't seen them.'

'We've made it, haven't we?'

'Almost,' the skipper said. 'We're getting close to the section of the river where we began. But there's one last obstacle. Look.'

Still groggy, Matt screwed up his eyes to look ahead.

A bar of sand stretched in a long line across

the river.

'What's that?'

'The final barrier. A sandbar. Not very wide, but it's right across the river so there's no way we can go around it.'

'You mean we've come this far only to find ourselves shut inside the river?'

'Afraid so.'

Matt looked up at the late afternoon sky. He remembered the words of the lockmaster:

'One final warning. Time is also your enemy. You have only twenty-four hours. You must go back to where you started, before you dropped the coin . . . to that afternoon so long ago when it all began, or here you must stay — locked in time!'

It seemed to be such a spiteful turn of events, one last attempt to hold them. Was it time to give up?

Matt thought of his father and mother and Bexie waiting for him. He thought of Emma Jane and her dreams of the future:

'I want to go ahead with you. I want my future. I want to grow up and have a life. . .'

Had he journeyed through four locks of

time, faced a river of snags, of weeping willows, misty uncertainties and surprises, including a flood, a stranding and a race against a ghost paddleboat, to give up now?

He knew that he couldn't give up. They must find a way to overcome this last obstacle. He must undo the nightmare he began when he dropped the coin into the box.

'We're running out of time,' Matt said. 'We're going to have to chance it. We'll have to send her at the sandbank at full speed and hope our momentum carries us over. But we'll have to go as fast as we can.'

'We're already at full speed,' the skipper said, glancing at the telegraph.

'I know how to get three or four more horsepower out of the engine,' Matt said.

'It's going to be risky. It'll be the engine or the sandbar,' the skipper said warningly.

'It'll be the sandbar or us,' Matt said. 'See you later.' Then he added, 'I hope.' Jamie would have been proud of him.

Matt dragged the diminished pile of redgum logs to the edge of the engine pit, then tumbled them over the edge. He scrambled down the companionway, his eardrums cringing at the clatter of the engine and the shriek that he knew would come.

When he opened the firebox door and

crammed the logs inside the furnace heat, blasted against his face. He banged the door shut and waited, watching the pressure gauge climb. An upward glance showed him Emma Jane standing at the rail at the edge of the landing pit, looking down. Jamie came down the ladder to join him. Together, in silent, fascinated suspense, they watched the pressure gauge mount.

The safety valve went off with a splitting shriek and the *Return* hit the sandbank — the final barrier in the final lock of time.

Time warped in the heat of the engine pit.

There was a blinding flash and then the world went quiet:

> *'Here,' Jamie said, handing a coin hastily to Matt as if it were burning his palm. 'I really think you should have the fun of starting it. I suppose.'*
>
> *'Be careful,' the girl said. 'Put that coin in there and start her engine and who knows where the* Return *will take us. Maybe she will take us back into the past.'*
>
> *Matt took the money between two fingers and held it over the slot in the coin box. He hesitated. The coin flared in a beam of afternoon sun that found its way into the engine pit.*

Time and eternity blended.

He looked at Jamie. His eyes were alight, like reflections in coins. He looked at the girl. Her fingers clenched around the rail that ran around the engine pit. The fingers tensed, whitened.

Matt's fingers locked, wouldn't part.

Matt's fingers closed around the coin as he refused to drop it.

'This must go back where it belongs,' he said.

They were back on the static museum display of the *Return!*

*   *   *

Matt's father appeared at the top of the engine pit.

'There you are.' He was wearing that skipper's hat, but Matt didn't think it looked so dumb any more. 'Glad you didn't steam off without me.'

Matt and Jamie climbed up the metal companionway.

'Just imagine if we had,' Emma Jane said.

'Love your costume,' his dad said.

'We're the friends of the PS *Return*,' she told him.

'We certainly are,' Matt agreed, smiling at her. 'All of us.'

'Do you know, I'll swear I can smell scones

baking,' Matt's father said.

'You can. Would you like a Devonshire tea?' Emma Jane asked, smiling brightly.

'You've won me,' Matt's father said. 'What about you two boys?'

'I wouldn't mind. I'd love some scones,' Jamie said.

'Me too,' added Matt. 'I'll bet Emma Jane makes the best scones in the world.'

They followed her to the galley.

'Glad you came,' Matt said to his father, and he meant it. His father put his arm around his shoulder.

'I've got a feeling we're going to enjoy the rest of this holiday, Matt. What do you think?'

'I know it,' Matt agreed. 'I'm looking forward to the future. All of it.'

'Me too,' his father said.

'I'm looking forward to the scones,' said Jamie.

15

Back in the flow

MATT STOOD NEXT to his father at the driving console of the houseboat.

They paddled along in bright morning sunshine. 'I've got Emma Jane's address,' he told his father. 'And Jamie's. I'm going to write,' he said. 'Emma Jane has promised to write. And Jamie will write too. He thinks.'

Sometimes it wasn't how long you knew friends that made them important, Matt thought. He had a feeling that these friends would play a part in his future.

'It's nice when everything's nice, isn't it?' his mother said. She was playing a game of cards with Bexie on a small table in the lounge area.

'Yes, it is,' Matt said. 'And things are pretty good right now, aren't they?'

'They couldn't get much better,' his father said. 'They could only change and be happy in different ways. And we shouldn't be afraid of that, I suppose. You were right when you said that we can't live in the past.'

'You were also right when you said the future comes all too soon and we shouldn't be in a rush to join it,' Matt said. 'From now on I'm going to enjoy things as they come.'

They rounded a bend. The river stretched ahead of them, shining in the morning sun.

It was perfect.